Craven Street

Also By E.J. Stevens

Whitechapel Paranormal Society
Craven Street

Ivy Granger Psychic Detective
Frostbite
Shadow Sight
Blood and Mistletoe
Ghost Light
Club Nexus
Burning Bright
Birthright
Devil in the Details
Hound's Bite
Thrill on Joysen Hill
Tales from Harborsmouth

Hunters' Guild
Hunting in Bruges

Spirit Guide
She Smells the Dead
Spirit Storm
Legend of Witchtrot Road
Brush with Death
The Pirate Curse

Poetry
From the Shadows
Shadows of Myth and Legend

Craven Street

E.J. Stevens

Published by Sacred Oaks Press
Sacred Oaks, 221 Sacred Oaks Lane, Wells, Maine 04090

First Printing (trade paperback edition), June 2019

Stevens, E.J.
Craven Street/ E.J. Stevens

ISBN 978-1-946046-36-9 (trade pbk.)

Printed in the United States of America

PUBLISHER'S NOTE
This is a work of fiction. Names, characters, places, and incidents either are the product of the author's imagination or are used fictitiously, and any resemblance to actual persons, living or dead, business establishments, events, or locales is entirely coincidental.

FLIGHT FROM THE ROOKERY

Cora

Chapter 1

I squinted at the address from the evening's dispatch, struggling to decipher the building number in the eternal darkness of Thrawl Street. Like most of the East End, gas lamps here were few and far between, leaving Whitechapel's residents and visitors stumbling in a quagmire of fog, smoke, and shadow.

The conditions were rife for the wicked dealings of man and inhuman beast alike, though my finer dress and reputation for charitable good works, both mundane and supernatural, had seen me safely through many nocturnal ramblings. Not that I took my safety for granted. Being set upon by thieves was but one possibility.

In recent weeks, we'd seen an uptick in natterings about spectral activity and more than one credible case of demonic possession. Something had agitated the city's spectral citizens and underworld denizens alike. The presence of demons was particularly vexing and, though the dispatch indicated a possible ghost sighting, I'd be a fool to assume that the night held only the threat of a simple banishing ritual.

My eyes scanned the narrow street, flicking to the intersection of Brick Lane to the east and the barely discernable crossroads with George Street to the west. The street was barely wide enough for two women to walk abreast, a feature that added to my unease. It would be far too easy to become trapped here between these deteriorating buildings. Their moldy brick and stone façades, gangrenous in the half-light, the last thing I'd see before the curtain of death fell.

I considered my decision to forego a position considered suitable for a young lady, but shook off the thought with a snort. I hadn't the patience or skill of a dressmaker, nor the inclination to become a dutiful wife. Working for the Special Paranormal Research Branch might require quicker wits and a stronger stomach than the aforementioned options, but it was never dull.

The Special Paranormal Research Branch, a secret group of talented men and women working within the British police force, was created to monitor and gauge paranormal threats. I was part of an all-female unit with a success rate so high that we'd had more than one letter of gratitude from the queen.

Unfortunately, my unit's successes had done nothing to put us in the favor of our male counterparts. Working outside the home, especially doing work that put us within close proximity to the darker side of the human and inhuman condition, was felt to be unsuitable for women. Saving Queen and country from demons, ghouls, and angry spirits was socially unacceptable, scandalous even.

So, with righteous fury and considerable displeasure, our male colleagues tried to make our work unbearable. Indeed, it was obvious even to the least observant that our male colleagues expected us to quit. We were repeatedly assigned the most abominable cases, frequently forced to walk Whitechapel's tortuous and twisted streets. Not that it stopped us.

Through patronizing smiles and tedious sneers, we'd been labeled the Whitechapel Paranormal Society, as if we were no more than a sewing circle or a charitable group. But instead of quitting, we embraced the moniker, going so far as to use our "society" as a cover for our movements throughout the East End. It was astonishing the places a group of Spiritualists are permitted to venture. No soul wants to anger a restless spirit or those whom they believe to command them.

Not that we traveled unmolested. Whitechapel was rife with violent crime, both human and paranormal. For that reason, we usually traveled in pairs. But we'd suffered a recent loss, leaving us at sixes and sevens. As special sergeant, the safety of my constables was my responsibility. Which left me on my own to investigate a possible supernatural disturbance, a situation I was regretting as I caught sight of the same dirt-besmeared walls I'd passed thrice already.

During my years with the S.P.R.B., I'd learned to find my way about the East End's warrens, but I dare say the Flower and Dean rookery put even my navigational skills to the test. I'd lost the final hours of daylight searching that labyrinthine warren for the lodging house where guests had allegedly been terrorized by a ghostly apparition.

It was only with the most prodigious luck that I tilted my head back in exasperation, bringing the small, grimy plaque into sight. A grin slid across my face and I strode straight for the shadowed doorway below the sign.

In for a penny, in for a pound. I lifted a gloved hand and rang the bell.

Chapter 2

The man's scowl and furrowed brow held a barely restrained air of menace that stole the breath from my lungs and had me reaching for the dagger hidden within my voluminous skirts.

"Four pence for a bed, tuppence for the rope," he said.

I tried not to bristle at the suggestion I appeared to be of such low condition as to only have a tuppence. Joining the Special Paranormal Research Branch had seen an advantageous rise in my station, but even my parents, who'd lived a life in service, would have had the means for a bed. I smiled, baring my teeth.

"Cora Drummond of the Whitechapel Paranormal Society," I said, handing the proprietor of the lodging house my calling card. "I'm not in need of a bed, sir. I've come with regard to reports of a spiritual disturbance."

His brow furrowed even more as he squinted in the crepuscular light. I held my breath, but he nodded, seemingly satisfied. The motion drew attention to a bald spot that sat in a greasy, black sea of untidy hair that stuck out in every direction. His unkempt state and malmsey nose suggested a fondness for drink, but his eyes held a clear, calculating intelligence.

The man was a troublesome conundrum. And had I imagined him grinning maliciously, or had that been a trick of the light? Suddenly alert, I checked that my purse was secure and my dagger was close to hand.

"We've been expectin' you, miss," he said with a self-congratulatory clap of his hands. "Right this way."

I jumped slightly at the explosive sound, but followed the flophouse proprietor past a guttering gaslight and into a parlor with little more than an armchair. Beside it sat a small tray holding a congealing bowl of half-eaten eel jelly. It would seem I'd disturbed this man's supper.

Perhaps that was why he'd appeared in such foul humor upon my arrival. I let out a brief exhale. Things would go much more smoothly with this man's cooperation. As if to prove the direction of my thoughts, he reached for the tray and motioned for me to sit.

"Let me fetch ye' a cuppa," he said.

I nodded and he lumbered away, disappearing to what must fulfill the role of kitchen in this squalid tenement. I wasn't eager to drink anything the odious man offered, but the ritual of tea would do much to breach the gap toward civility. If there was an angry spirit on the premises, it was my sworn duty to banish it and protect the innocent humans residing here.

I waited, but the landlord didn't return from the kitchen. I paced the confining space of the parlor, wondering if the reports of spectral activity had been nothing more than a ruse, a prank to play on a group of privileged Spiritualists. A scuff of boot on floorboards came from the direction of the gloomy doorway and the hair on the back of my neck stood on end.

A mass of limbs lurched from the sheltering darkness beyond. Distorted, leering faces flashed into view, setting my heart to race. From within their grimacing lips erupted an unnerving, malevolent moan that filled me with dread. Nostrils burning with the acrid stench of brimstone, I wrinkled my nose and sought the nearest exit.

With great urgency, I ran. Stomach roiling, I slid across the uneven flooring of the outer hallway. I caught the doorframe with an out-flung hand and thrust myself down a hallway and toward the door that led to the street and freedom.

Unfortunate tenants poured from the crowded rooms and connecting passageways like roaches, eyes gleaming with an infernal hunger as they lurched toward me.

"We are legion."

Chapter 3

"**M**ary, mother of god," I muttered.

The unfortunates residing within the rat-like warren of Wilmott's Lodging House had become the unwitting hosts for a multitude of demons powerful enough to break through the barriers between Hell and the earthly plane. It wasn't unheard of for one or two demons to break the chains of their confinement, either through intentional summoning or by table-knocking misadventure, but this was unimaginable lunacy.

Sadly, no matter how preposterous, a horde of innocent men and women possessed by demons was still hot on my heels. Thaumaturgical theories would have to wait.

In a daring act of utter impropriety, I lifted my skirts and tied them at the hip. Cheeks burning, I ran with the singular goal of reaching safety, or, barring that, at least a defensible position. My team maintains a nearby bolt-hole, but whether or not I could reach it unmolested was debatable.

I tightened my grip on my dagger and forced my free hand to refrain from fiddling with my dress. Now that the initial shock had worn off, I was increasingly aware of my current state of disarray. For once, I was thankful for the gloom of London's East End. But that relief was short-lived as I strained to locate my pursuers over my own labored breathing.

A scraping of boots over stone and a sinister, sibilant moan was all the incentive I needed to force a final burst of speed. Choking and gasping for air, I spun hard and disappeared into a narrow passageway to my left. I flew down the dark alley, navigating its labyrinthine twists, warren of alcoves, and bizarre outcroppings of wood and brick with gloved hands slick with malodorous grime.

It was behind one of these seemingly random outcroppings of brick that I ducked, gripping my dagger and holding my breath. I bit my lip and listened for footfalls. After a count to ten, I risked a glance around the corner, unable to trust my sense of hearing over the rushing of blood in my ears.

My stomach churned, but I saw no sign of pursuers. With a silent prayer, I ducked behind the wall, felt for a slender gap in the brickwork, and slipped into a hidden stairway. I took the stairs two at a time, reaching the landing and its wooden door in seconds. I unlocked the door with shaking hands, listened one final time for my pursuers, and hurried inside.

I leaned hard against the door, drawing in gulps of stale air heavy with the scent of my teammates. Normally, I'd find the acrid remnants of Flan's cigars layered with Edith's oppressive floral perfume an annoyance, but in my current predicament the smells were comforting.

With a shallow sigh, I moved unhurried to the mantle. I pocketed my dagger, struck a match, and lit a candle, blinking as my eyes adjusted to the light. A quick survey of the room showed that it was as I'd left it the morning after a tête-à-tête and subsequent kiss that still made my stomach flutter. What the devil had I been thinking?

I shook my head, dispelling the memory. It was best to focus on the problem at hand. I licked my lips and went to the sideboard and poured myself a restorative.

Brandy sloshed onto my wrist, alerting me to the terrible state of my attire. Running blindly down narrow, filthy streets and alleys had done a number on my clothing. I peeled off gloves that were now soiled and torn beyond repair, tossing them in the rubbish bin.

I rubbed damp hands down the front of my dress and winced. Apparently, I'd damaged more than mere cloth in my flight through Whitechapel. I bared my palms to the candle flame, wrinkling my nose at the bloody scratches mottled with dark effluvium.

I began scrubbing and bandaging my hands, aware that I was fortunate. While not entirely unscathed, I'd escaped the horde of demons that had been residing at Wilmott's Lodging House. It was obvious that the assignment had been a trap. Whether the goal had been to kill or to capture a Spiritualist was uncertain.

An even more troubling thought wormed its way into my thoughts, and I set down the roll of cloth bandage. Heaven forbid our enemy was aware of and had targeted the Special Paranormal Research Branch. No, that was preposterous.

We all took an inviolable oath of secrecy and service to Queen and country. Only a madman would break such a solemn promise.

I reached for the decanter, preparing to pour another glass of brandy, and froze. Had thoughts of demons stoked the flames of my imagination? But no, the sound came again. Heavy footsteps tread on the landing outside the door.

I retrieved a revolver from the mantle, steadied my aim, and blew out the candle.

Chapter 4

The door swung open to display a tall, lithe figure holding a wicked blade. The outline of trousers and wool cap barely discernible, backlit only by the hallway gas lamp.

The intruder's face was completely obscured by shadow, but the clink of bottles and jaunty way the person leaned against the doorframe set my mind at ease. I let out a sigh of relief and struck a match.

"What are you doing here?" I asked, busying myself relighting the candle.

I kept my back to Flan, delaying meeting her eyes. The problem with working closely with a team of psychics, even those with minor, unpredictable abilities, was that on occasion they saw through my steely façade, their talent bearing forth a weakness I didn't wish to make claim to. Flan's psychic ability was particularly distressing.

I put away the revolver and cursed.

Flan was an exceptionally vexing double-edged sword. Her masculine manner of dress gave her an uncanny ability to infiltrate nearly any unsavory gang of hooligans, allowing her to go wherever and do whatever she pleased. That freedom added to her skill with a blade and total disregard for her own health made Flan a logical rival for leadership. Not that our unit's pecking order was ever truly in question. For all her fine qualities, Flan reveled in a passionate pursuit of independence that included flouting the very rules that made a good leader.

Most annoyingly, in addition to her disregard for rules and inclination for heroics, Flan could pick up on emotions. It wasn't infallible, but, more often than not, if a team member was in peril, she sensed it. Her awareness of my recent fear and her sudden appearance led me to the uncomfortable conclusion that she'd once again peered inside my heart and come to my aid. That knowledge set my teeth on edge.

"I don't need saving," I said, pounding a fist on the mantle.

I turned to face her as she shut the door. Flan shrugged and flopped into the nearest chair.

"Who said anything about saving?" she said, thrusting a leg over the arm of the chair with an air of indifference. "I'm just here for the hooch."

She took a swig off the open bottle in her hand, finishing off the noxious liquid within, as if to illustrate her point.

"You're telling me that you happened to be in proximity to this bolt-hole and ran out of drink at the same time that I took refuge here?" I asked, voice raising with incredulity.

"Is that so hard to believe?" she asked, eyes twinkling.

Fists tight, fingernails biting into bandaged palms, I growled through clenched teeth.

"What are you really doing here, Flan?" I asked.

She tossed the empty bottle in the bin, grabbed a new bottle of whiskey from the sideboard to her left, waved the bottle in a rolling motion, and raised her eyebrows questioningly. Defeated, I threw my hands in the air and nodded. Flan passed me a glass with two fingers of whiskey.

"The real question is, why are you here, Cora?" she asked, leaning forward.

"I had a case to investigate," I said, intentionally vague.

"Spectral activity in the Flower and Dean rookery, possible poltergeist," she said.

I frowned and set the untouched glass of whiskey on the mantle.

"Yes, the level of activity mentioned in the dispatch suggested poltergeist," I said.

"But it wasn't a mere ghost, was it?" she asked.

"I'm sure I don't know what you mean," I said.

"Poppycock," she said. "It wasn't a ghost, was it?

"No," I said, shaking my head. "It wasn't. But how on earth did you know?"

"You're not easily frightened, Cora," she said, tapping her head. So, it had been her psychic ability after all. "I felt your fear. There is no way you panicked over a poltergeist, not even a strong one. Anna, sure. Lottie or Edith, maybe. But not you."

I lifted my chin, a strange mixture of pride, pleasure, and gratitude swelling my chest. It was rare to be seen as anything other than frail when you are of the so-called weaker sex.

"You're right," I said, lips tugging in a wry grin. "It wasn't a poltergeist. It was a gods be damned trap."

Chapter 5

"Mass possession," Flan said, running a hand through unruly hair.

The motion knocked her wool cap askew and my fingers flexed, wanting to set it to rights. I growled at the impulse and started to pace the length of the room. Flan's hat wasn't the only thing off kilter. Indeed, the entire world seemed to be at a dangerous tilt, careening through a maelstrom toward unspeakable horrors.

"If I hadn't seen it with my own eyes…" I said with a shrug.

"Damn, Cora," she said, voice rough. "You reek of brimstone. I can smell the truth on you. And yet…"

"…and yet it's utterly preposterous," I said.

I met her gaze, holding it for a heartbeat too long. Her eyes slid down and a grin tugged her lips.

"Can't say I mind the new look," she said with a wink. "You should run from demons more often."

My cheeks burned, belatedly reminded of my state of dress. I fumbled with my skirts, the knot I'd made during my flight from the Flower and Dean rookery holding fast. I drew my dagger, ready to stab the treasonous tangle of fabric, when a shadow fell over the blade and a hand settled on mine.

"Let me," Flan said.

Despite her manner of dress, Flan's hands were surprisingly delicate. They were also extremely agile, skilled as they were in the art of pickpocketing and lockpicking.

I stood transfixed as her pale, slender fingers undid the knot.

"There," she said, dropping the fabric and stepping away.

Her voice was gentle, but I retreated and resumed my pacing. This was no time for distractions or introspection. The safety of the realm was at stake. I'd have plenty of time to examine petty emotions after we stamp out the demonic infestation plaguing London's East End.

Assuming we survived.

"Now that decorum has been restored," I said, ignoring Flan's snort. "I suggest we tackle the problem at hand. Namely, how the devil any mere mortal managed to summon more than a dozen demons, beasts strong enough to enter the earthly realm and take full possession of their unfortunate hosts."

"A séance gone wrong?" she suggested. "Some kind of accidental summoning ritual? It's unlikely one man or woman, no matter how gifted, could have managed to bring that many demons across. And for what purpose? A demon deal? Everyone knows those bargains are best made at crossroads, and I've never heard of it requiring more than one demon to do the foul deed."

Flan's mention of a séance gave me an idea for a possible solution. Of course, it was a terrible idea that could most certainly go wrong in a multitude of ways.

While not the typical table-knocking one thinks of from a medium, I had a unique ability up my sleeve. I couldn't open the door to the Summerland, but I was a conduit of sorts. Keenly aware of the danger plaguing our patch of London, I ignored the rising dread that twisted my insides. We needed information, no matter how unsavory the source.

"There is one way," I said.

"You can't be serious," she said.

"I am deadly serious," I said.

I stopped pacing in front of a mirror that hung near the room's wash basin and makeshift sleeping chambers. Dread ran spidery fingers up my spine, but I leaned forward and exhaled, my breath fogging the silvered surfaced. Rather than retreating, the fog grew, swallowing my reflection.

I shivered, the temperature in the room plummeting. Despite the fire I'd set roaring in the grate while telling Flan the story of my flight from Thrawl Street, I had to fight off a chill seeping into my bones. Frost rimed the edges of the mirror, icy veins spreading otherworldly corruption. The icy tendrils curved and twisted, racing toward each other and when they met, the mirror cracked.

I reached for the mirror and wiped a hand across its surface, exposing an impenetrable darkness. I swallowed hard, bracing myself for what was to come. I didn't have to wait long.

"Bloody hell," Flan muttered.

A figure strode elegantly out of the darkness, stalking toward the mirror's surface. The urge to flee, to grab Flan and run, was undeniably strong. The man, for there was something singularly male about the figure, was menacing. For all his elegance, there was always the sense of a predator stalking its prey.

As he came closer, a face coalesced from the shadows and fog. It was a face that haunted my dreams, a face of almost painful beauty, a face that promised secrets if only I would listen.

The sad fact was, I had listened all too often. As a child, I'd caught his dazzling smiling face in every reflective surface. Whether I was polishing the silver, passing by a looking glass, or splashing in a puddle, he was there, my own secret prince.

"My lady, Cora," he said with a mocking bow.

"Jonathan," I said, chin lifted to meet his shifting gaze.

I'd grown older and wiser, and learned from the folly of innocence, but my immaterial friend, though not the prince or faithful servant that he professed, did serve a purpose. Laced within his lies, he always gifted me with a seed of truth. It was weeding out the deceptions that was tricky, which was why, though I was loath to admit it, I was grateful for Flan's steady presence.

"Tell me a story," I said. "Tell me about the unfortunate souls possessed by demons, the ones who followed me this evening. Tell me what manner of man could summon such a horde, and to what foul purpose."

Chapter 6

"Do you believe that…that thing?" Flan asked.

I shook my head, still unable to speak. I'd hoped that Jonathan, whatever he was, would throw light on the situation. Instead, I had the nagging suspicion that all he'd done was bloody the already murky waters.

I tipped back my glass, thankful for the burn as whiskey hit my throat. It would excuse the traitorous tears welling behind my eyelids.

"I'm afraid so," I said, finally finding my voice. "Some of what he said at least. Although I'm at a loss as to what our next move should be."

Jonathan had suggested, with the sibilant whispers and twists and turns of labyrinthine stories as was his way, that the incident in the rookery was only the beginning. The demonic summoning and mass possession were but an early manifestation of power, a testing of and mastery over a form of sorcery whose source was a well of evil deeper and darker than anything the Special Paranormal Research Branch had ever faced before.

The fiend had so enjoyed the exchange. Indeed, the man had relished burdening us with the terrifying tale. His gleeful grin still burned in my mind.

"You're sure he can't hear us?" Flan asked, casting a wary, suspicious glance at the mirror.

"He's gone," I said.

Banishing Jonathan was the one psychic skill I'd managed to finally master.

Whether our abilities were gifted at birth or triggered by illness or trauma, every member of my team had struggled with gaining control over our psychic gifts. Flan had sought to focus intruding on only the emotions of our team, Edith St. Germaine had honed her truth-telling skills to a frightening, razor-sharp accuracy, Lottie could read tea leaves and dowse for spectral activity with some precision, and even little Anna's healing gifts were becoming more reliable. But we'd all started out with erratic gifts we couldn't truly count on, gifts that left us vulnerable.

I knew that all too well. Being unable to control manifesting a presence, especially one as menacing and troublesome as Jonathan, was a liability. It wasn't sufficient to banish his shadowy silhouette in the mirror. I had to cut the connection entirely, banishing him back to the dark realm from which he came. I shivered, aware of the many years the creature had watched and listened, spying on my vulnerable, child self without restriction. It was a violation that I would not soon forget.

"Oh, Cora," Flan said, setting a hand on my arm. "You weren't to know."

I shook her off and leapt from my chair, unwilling to be mollycoddled. This was a time for action.

"Come!" I shouted over my shoulder, pocketing the revolver from the mantle.

I sloughed off Flan's sympathy, burning away the final remnants of cold and lethargy with decisive forward movement. I was the leader of our team, the sergeant in charge of four constables. Our numbers might currently be diminished, but not the weight of our responsibility nor our oath.

I raced down the stairs and through a warren of narrow alleyways, bursting out onto the roar and clatter of Whitechapel High Street. I hailed a hansom cab, startling the driver with my intensity. Flan jumped in behind me without hesitation, turning to me with a wide grin as she rapped with a cane she'd seized along the way.

"To Buckingham Palace," I shouted. "And drive like the devil."

ALONG CAME A DEMON

Forneus

Chapter 7

I sniffed, wincing at the foul stench of humanity. I narrowed my eyes, peering over the lace handkerchief, watching the ebb and flow of tainted souls with a keen eye as they passed before me on the narrow street.

Collecting human souls is a thankless job, nearly as tedious as acting as solicitor to the fae. Sadly, I, Forneus Grand Marquis of Hell, am currently reduced to performing both duties in servitude to my master, his lordship who shall not be named. Never play cards with one of The Fallen, I daresay, not unless you enjoy spending a millennium in indentured labor to a bilious, old fool.

I'd come to London to settle a dispute between a fetch and a banshee, but after a month spent listening to an endless litany of supposed crimes and misdemeanors between the rival faeries, I'd had enough. A demon lord can only tolerate so many mind-numbingly boring territorial disputes before going quite mad.

Doubtless, they'd rack up even more claims of wrongful death portents against one another in my absence, but I needed a change of scenery. So, I swapped the weeping willows and mausoleums of Highgate Cemetery for the gambling halls and opium dens of Limehouse and Whitechapel.

It was a testament to mankind's willful depravity that the men in these dark corners of London, whether they be members of the peerage out for an evening of slumming or resident dockside ruffians, smelled worse than their deceased neighbors to the north. The malodorous weed of the opium dens wasn't the only dark, fetid thing clinging to their physical bodies. Sickly, jaundiced souls trailed behind men on tattered, moth-eaten tethers, rife for the plucking.

I licked my lips, handkerchief disappearing into my waistcoat with a flick of the wrist. I could use magical trickery to ensnare these souls, but where was the fun in that?

I slipped into the sluggish flow of humanity, walking jauntily toward a dockside establishment, daring thugs and thieves with a rakish smile. Perhaps, I'd be fortunate enough to need the blade hidden inside the ebony cane I swung lazily at my side. These streets held dangers for a well-dressed man about town.

Sadly, I made it to my destination without need for a deadly perambulatory accessory. More's the pity.

Men who were truly evil, the ones who profited from the suffering of others, were always the most delicious. There was even a time when I might have had more empathy toward the plight of men ensnared by circumstance and lack of opportunity, feasting only on their oppressors, but those days were gone. My heart was hardened, and I was a better servant for it, but I was *dreadfully* bored.

I sighed and began my descent, stepping gingerly over more than one body slumped on the steep flight of stairs. Once inside, I received a portion of drug from the attendant. With a nod, I moved deeper into the hovel, stalking toward the walls where men lay stacked like sacks of grain on wooden berths.

Most visitors would require a moment for their eyes to adjust to the stygian darkness broken only by flickers of flame and smoldering embers. But most visitors didn't happen to be a demon. A chuckle escaped my lips, mingling with the broken sobs, malignant laughter, delirious sighs, and incoherent mumbling of those in the arms of Morpheus.

I'd worried that this excursion would be laced with the same oppressive tedium of the previous fortnight's legal transactions, that is until I spotted my prey. A man with mutton-chop whiskers, hair slicked with pomade, and dressed in a stylish frock coat moved stealthily toward a curtained back room. I caught the flash of a signet ring as he glanced over his shoulder and ducked into a candlelit private room beyond.

Deceiving such a man would be far more satisfying than the child's play of robbing limp, drug-addled fools of their souls. Many a man here would happily trade his own mother for the portion of drug I now pocketed. That was all well and good for fulfilling quotas but did nothing to break the monotony of immortality.

I leaned forward, listening, taking pleasure in drawing out the moment. Was that a woman's voice behind the curtain? Were those snarls and mutterings also coming from the private room? Most curious.

I would soon join the gentleman in his secret assignation. I breathed deeply and shuddered in anticipation. Did the curtain hide a hideous perversion, a sinister scheme, or a tale of squandered inheritance? How terribly interesting.

I would not miss it for the world.

THE SO-CALLED WEAKER SEX

Cora

Chapter 8

"Her Majesty is not currently in residence," said the footman blithely.

I knew the statement to be false, my office received regular reports on the queen's whereabouts as it was the only way to ensure the safety of the realm, but I nodded, strangling my reticule rather than the messenger.

"Of course, sir," I said. "Thank you, sir."

It wasn't until I was once again safely ensconced within the curtained carriage, and on our way to our offices, that I swore.

"Blood hell," I muttered.

"It didn't go well, I presume?" Flan asked, eyebrow lifting inquisitively.

I repositioned the bench cushions roughly, face burning, more than willing to vent my spleen on the carriage's unfortunate upholstery. In fact, I was sorely tempted to lift a cushion to my face and scream into its musty depths.

"No, I was not received," I said, biting off the words.

"Idiots," she swore.

"Flan, not now," I said, raising my fingertips to massage my temples.

We remained awkwardly silent, the clatter of hooves our only company until we disembarked at the Vauxhall Club, the cover for S.P.R.B.'s secret offices. Of course, we couldn't enter the front entrance, an endless source of amusement for our male colleagues. I wrapped my shawl tighter about my shoulders and stalked to the servant's entrance.

Heaven forefend a group of gifted women grace the illustrious halls of such a place. Edith, one of my constables, vociferously held the belief that gentlemen's clubs, and their patriarchal rules of membership, were the work of the devil. We didn't see eye to eye on much, but on this we were in wholehearted agreement. Sadly, a secret club was an excellent front for a policing branch that did not publicly exist.

I scowled as I pushed past the overly hot kitchens and through a side door into the lobby. I was deep in thought, chewing over the troubling prospect of organizing a mass exorcism in the Flower and Dean rookery, when something in Flan's tone at my shoulder brought me up sharp.

"The gossipmongers within the Yard, or at least within Special Branch, have been hard at work, I see," Flan muttered, voice low.

I couldn't see what had put the steely edge into Flan's voice. She was easily a head taller than me, even in her less fashionable footwear.

I hastened to clear the veritable jungle of potted ferns blocking my view, stiffening and going still when the wide expanse of corkboard came within sight. Constables and clerks used the board to communicate duty rosters, district coverage, news of a supernatural nature throughout the city, and case-related bulletins.

It was also where sergeant, nay, *Inspector* Snidely-Moore, attempted to publicly humiliate me and the members of my unit. Lysander Snidely-Moore and his men posting unflattering depictions of agents of the so-called weaker sex, of which we were the only female agents in all the Special Paranormal Research Branch, had become a frequent means of torment. They used it as a stage upon which to voice their most baseless, and base, beliefs.

What ridiculous confabulation did they presume now?

It didn't matter that, as a sergeant, Snidely-Moore had left Limehouse's K-division under a cloud, or that he wore evidence of the previous night's debauchery, mainly drinking, gambling, whoring, and illegal fisticuffs, like a badge of honor. I found the smudges of rouge, splashes of cheap wine, bloodied knuckles, and the telltale pink paper of The Sporting Times peeking from his pocket all rather nauseating.

Although, the fingernail gashes along his neck, not quite hidden by his overcompensatingly large mutton-chop whiskers, gave me some small satisfaction. Still, the knowledge that he'd been promoted to inspector, faster than me no less, was preposterous. The man was a lout.

Feeling peevish, I turned on my heel to get a better view of the board and whatever vile post it had on display. I snarled, hands flexing, ignoring the sharp pain of my corset at the involuntary puffing of my chest. It would do me no good to become apoplectic. They'd blame me of succumbing to a case of the vapors, only more evidence of my fragility and inability to lead. But one hand slid to my pocket, my fingers resting on the warm, reassuring weight of my revolver.

They'd drawn my likeness atop the savagely mutilated body of a corpse.

It was unthinkable.

Even more unimaginable, was the bulletin beside the vile photograph informing us that a male inspector, Inspector Snidely-Moore to be exact, had been assigned to investigate the faceless victim, a corpse found on my patch.

"This is an outrage," I said through clenched teeth.

"'bout time the powers that be done somethin' sensible like," Snidely-Moore said, tipping his bowler hat mockingly with one meaty hand while grabbing at his manhood with the other.

The smell of onions, tobacco, and cheap wine made my stomach churn.

"Shut your bone box, Snidely-Moore," Flan said menacingly.

A quick glance showed what I suspected; Flan was not so innocently cleaning the grime from beneath her fingernails with the tip of a dagger. While not overt, the threat she conveyed was real, indeed. Flan was a considerable foe with any blade. Snidely-Moore knew it, and so did his men.

"Heard you already had your hands full, missy, what with your supposed 'mass possession' in the rookery," Snidely-Moore said, making another rude gesture with his hand.

Flan let out a strangled hiss, low and predatory, but I shook my head. She stopped her prowling, surprising Snidely-Moore with how close she'd snuck up on him. Flan was good at that. Being forged in the crucible of a childhood spent on Whitechapel's streets had made my constable light on her feet and stealthy as a puma. It also made her viciously protective of those she considered family.

I raised a hand and tore the photo and the bulletin from the board. I narrowed my eyes, seeing where chalk and quick lime had been used to deface the original orders.

"This is our case, not yours," I said, lifting my chin.

He towered over me with his bulk, but I wasn't cowed. I'd had enough of the repulsive man and his condescending pedantry.

Three of his constables stood at his back, clubs at the ready, for what I'd rather not consider, but he slapped his leg and let out a forced guffaw.

"Just a bit o' fun!" he chortled. His voice was filled with joviality, but no laughter reached his black, beady eyes.

I turned on my heel, heading to my office, trying not to betray the heavy weight of fatigue that now dragged at my limbs. It was only the calamitous crashing of a body into a large ceramic urn that made me glance over my shoulder to see Snidely-Moore arse over teakettle in the remains of a giant-leafed fern.

"Just a bit of fun, old chap" Flan said, thumb pushing back the brim of her cap to show the full extent of a feral grin. "Just a bit of fun."

My fingers tightened on the sheaf of papers in my hand as a matching grin slid across my face. Flan was utterly incorrigible. I shook my head and hastened my stride, leaving the lobby, and Snidely-Moore and his goons, behind.

I might have laughed along with Flan under different circumstances, but the image of my likeness on the dismembered corpse's body was burned indelibly into my mind. I clenched my jaw, forcing myself to ignore the ominous tingling at the nape of my neck. Just a bit of fun, indeed.

Chapter 9

"There the matter stands at present," I said, a shiver running up my spine despite the coal Flan had added to the stove that squatted in the corner of our office.

I looked around the table, enduring the keen stares from my constables. I met their looks of open curiosity and tried not to fidget. Having peculiar qualities often attracted similar attention, and the recent encounter with my childhood tormentor had left me raw, but more unsettling were the nods of credulity with which they received my report.

Something had been brewing in London's East End, something dark and supernatural. We'd all seen signs of that escalation, but it was only now that we put voice to a possible cabal, a group of men with a common dark purpose. How else to explain the mass demon possession in the Flower and Dean rookery?

"And now this," Edith said with a derisive sniff, waving disapprovingly at the photograph. "What Godless bestial creature could do such a thing?"

"I doubt God had much to do with it," Flan said drily.

"At least you're unharmed, miss," Lottie said, pushing a cup of tea into my bandaged hand.

"Are you sure you are alright?" Anna asked, wringing her tiny gloved hands in earnest. "I'm getting much better at healing, Miss Drummond. Truly, I am. I hardly get tired at all now."

Lottie patted the young girl's arm, but gave me a discrete shake of the head. Not that I'd missed the dark smudges under the child's eyes. Anna was eager, but earnestness would not replace training. At sixteen, she was still but a child, and none of us wished to despoil her childhood more than our work had already.

Margaret "Lottie" Beck towered over us, even while seated, her dress and shawl straining over wide shoulders. She was a mountain of muscle with a razor-sharp mind and a heart of gold. She'd discovered her gift for reading tea leaves, entrails, and bones while working as a cook, and it was in the alley behind a bakery where she still sometimes worked that she'd found little Anna Russell digging through discarded rotten fruit in a gutter that ran thick with sewage.

Lottie had taken Anna in and when she learned of the girl's healing abilities, she brought her to our offices in hopes that Anna might find a position with the S.P.R.B. rather than in the sculleries. Even dusted as she was with flour and sugar, I wouldn't mistake Lottie's maternal inclinations for fragility. Which is why I hadn't mentioned that the quality that my superiors felt most worth considering was the child's virtue. They'd given the girl to me to use as bait, a tool to lure out demons and other vile creatures. Instead, I'd demanded the mental exercises necessary to control her healing powers.

"Yes, I'm fine," I said, averting my gaze.

I shifted my focus to the dead woman and the brief report attached to the photograph. The victim was female, though it was hard to tell much more beyond that. There were no belongings, nay no clothing at all, and the corpse was missing any identifying extremities. Indeed, there were no limbs or head found about the crime scene.

"Well, I think we can all agree that this is clearly not a case of misadventure," Flan said, rolling her eyes at the scribbled notes and perverse suggestions of the police constable who stumbled upon the body.

"Is that sort of sordid thing even physically possible?" Edith sniffed, grimacing in disgust.

Knowing Edith St. Germaine and her righteous sensibilities, she was likely more repulsed by a suggestion of sexual impropriety than by the woman's brutal dismemberment.

"The fact this poor woman's limbs were removed from her torso with such precision should put paid to the notion of a nocturnal assignation gone awry, and any at all belief that what befell her was in any way her own fault, but we all know what the muckrakers will do if they catch whiff of that bobby's notes," I said. "Lottie, send a telegraph to his division chief ordering that they keep their mouths shut. I'll not bring shame on this woman, whoever she was, because a police constable would rather suggest some tawdry fantasy than believe that monsters, whether supernatural or flesh and blood, walk amongst us."

"Yes, sergeant," she said, nodding. "I'll bring Miss Anna with me. I've been meaning to teach her the telegraph machine."

While I was sure that Lottie was more interested in removing the child from the grisly case before us than teaching her the machine, I agreed. Once they left the room, I squinted at the photograph, frowning.

"Flan, hand me your glass," I said, holding out a gloved hand. I took the offered glass, examining what had appeared at first glance to be strangely uniform cuts and scrapes upon the body's hips, shoulders, and just above the navel. "Do you see these, here and here?"

"Bloody hell," Flan said. "Are those what I think they are?"

Edith raised her pince-nez and leaned in for a closer look, and a hand flew to cover her mouth. Her face had gone pale and waxy, and she swallowed hard. Flan reached over to pour a finger of whiskey into Edith's teacup, and for once there was no complaint.

The drink's bracing effect was immediate, color rising again in her cheeks. Edith quickly crossed herself, eyes wide. We three weren't particularly squeamish, but I could tell that, at that moment, we were together in our disquiet. What a closer examination of the body had revealed was utterly beyond the pale.

"Arcane sigils cut deeply into the body with such force as to more than once reveal bone," I said. "We'll need to consult the archives, but if I'm correct, those marks will match the Barnes Mystery of last year, marks that were deemed by the S.P.R.B. to be indicative of black magic."

"They took a woman into custody, didn't they?" Edith asked.

"Kate Webster, the maid," Flan said with a nod, staring at the ceiling as if the case report resided there. "Murdered her employer, the widow Julia Martha Thomas. Dismembered the body, boiled off what flesh she could in the laundry copper, and dumped the rest in the Thames. Far as I know, the head was never recovered."

"And you think there's a connection?" Edith asked, looking between us.

"It says here that our body, such as it is, was discovered down near the docks," I said, pointing to the spot on a map. "The arms, legs, and head were likely removed from the torso before the body was dumped since no blood was found at the scene. Our police constable may have been an idiot, but he did make mention of that."

"The river, the dismemberment...," Edith said, shaking her head. "But what of the markings on our Whitechapel body. The Barnes Mystery was quite the sensation at the time, I remember it was in all the papers, but I don't recall anything about sigils carved into those remains."

"The S.P.R.B. made sure those details were kept quiet, but a little birdie told me," I said.

"That little birdie happen to go by the name of Billie?" Flan asked, eyebrow raised.

Billie was an informant, and was, at times, an unlikely friend. I wouldn't out the housebreaker, especially not with something so tangled with the upper brass. I hadn't asked Billie how they came upon that bit of information. I didn't want to know.

"Edith, I need you to organize an exorcism at the Flower and Dean rookery," I said, ignoring Flan. Her rivalry with Billie could wait. "I'll have Lottie and Anna go through the archives, looking for more on arcane sigils and for anything we have on the Barnes Mystery."

"And you?" Edith asked, glancing between me and Flan.

"We'll check in with river patrol and visit the docks," I said.

"Could also ask around the local mudlarks," Flan said. "See if anyone's seen anything. Not unusual for them to find bodies that have gone in the river."

"You think there will be more murders?" Edith asked, hand clutching the silver cross at her neck. "More dismembered women tossed in the river?"

I stared at the map and the expanse of Whitechapel that ran along the Thames, a shiver traveling up my spine. The room had gone cold and the smell of fish was overwhelming. I carefully avoided looking at the dead girl dripping in the corner.

"I have a bad feeling the body the constable found was just the beginning."

Chapter 10

"It happened again," I said, clenching my fists.

"You saw the deceased?" Flan asked, voice overloud to my ears.

"Not here," I said, nodding toward the door.

Once outside, ensconced within the noisy tumult of carriages on cobbles, she took my arm and turned me around, putting us face to face.

"Was it like before?" she asked, worry lines forming in the shadow of her wool cap. "Were they just…lurking, waiting for your help?"

"She was waiting," I said, nodding slowly in agreement. "She also smelled of fish and was dripping onto the office carpet."

"Wait here, I'll only be a moment," she said, running back inside.

When Flan emerged, she gingerly held a handkerchief between thumb and index finger.

"What…?" I asked.

"The floor," she said, grimacing. "It was still wet. And the water, what I managed to retrieve of it, smells of fish and rot."

"Then I didn't imagine the ghost of a dead girl, did I?" I asked with a sigh.

I ran a hand over my face and pinched the bridge of my nose, a headache blooming behind my eyes.

"Not in the least," she said. "And the conditions were like before? They only manifest when all of us are in the room?"

I thought back to the icy draught and the moment the dead woman manifested from the ether.

"Yes," I said.

"Then we could recreate the conditions," she said excitedly. "Hold a proper séance. Edith has always held that your claims of not being a true medium are a lie."

"I'm no clairvoyant," I said. "I commune only with Jonathan, whoever or whatever he is."

"Then Agnes died," she said.

I stiffened, tears welling.

"I don't say this to hurt you, Cora, only to relay the facts," she said. "Either her power transferred to you, a parting gift perhaps, or the trauma of her loss triggered the change in you. Whatever the reason, the spirits of the dead have found you."

"And I can see them," I said.

"So it would seem," she said.

"Bugger."

Chapter 11

Although our focus was most often fixed upon Whitechapel, all of the East End, including Aldgate, Bethnal Green, Bow, Limehouse, Mile End, Shadwell, and Wapping, often fell within our team's purview. We were no strangers to the docklands, though going there could feel like venturing into another country.

At Flan's suggestion, we decided to begin our search at the London Docks and Shadwell Basin. There was a bend here in the River Thames that, when combined with currents and commerce, made this spot a natural collection point for all sorts of things that might find their way into the dark, murky waters. It was also a central launching point for our investigation with various mudlarks working along the river to the west and Limehouse to the east.

Deep in thought, I startled into alertness at the piercing shrill of a police whistle coming from the direction of the river. The sound was echoed from the docks, not far from where we stood. I met the eager gleam in Flan's eyes with a grin of my own.

In silent agreement, we ran, putting every ounce of energy into our pursuit.

"Oi!" a man bellowed.

Eyes wide, I pivoted at the last second, nearly tumbling over a pile of rope and into the water as we rounded a corner. Flan being more agile and less encumbered in her trousers, managed a dance-like move and a wink as she spun past me. My cheeks heated, but I laughed before we came to a halt before a stern-faced bobby.

"What is the trouble?" I asked, holding out my warrant card for his inspection. It received a familiar level of scrutiny and incredulity from the policeman which I chose to ignore. I turned my attention to Flan who was on tiptoes, attempting a view beyond a stack of crates. "Constable?"

"Someone's trying to fish something out of the river," she said. Flan turned to the copper. "Did one of the dockhands fall in?"

"No, sir," he said, frowning at Flan in confusion. "River patrol, Thames River Police that is, miss…er sir. They found somethin' peculiar-like."

"Let us through then, constable," I said, thrusting out my chin and forcing the authority of my office into my voice. "There is work to be done here."

He bit his lip but nodded and stepped aside. Better to allow us to pass and let the Thames Police be burdened with us. Flan flashed him a smile with too many teeth and then we were hurrying down the jetty where a uniformed man jumped from boat to dock while continuing to maneuver something in the water with a long barge pole.

We held out our warrant cards as we reached the man, but he didn't spare them a glance.

"If you are who you say, then grab me that net there and be quick about it," he said.

Flan held out the net and between the two of them they fished a large item out of the water. A cloth-wrapped bundle hit the wooden planks at our feet with a wet thud.

I wrinkled my nose, swallowing hard at the stench. The smell of fish and rot was the same as the dead girl who'd recently haunted our offices at S.P.R.B. headquarters. I daresay, it wasn't a coincidence.

"Don't go spoilin' the evidence," the man said. "Step away if you need to be sick."

The words were practical rather than cruel, a fact made clear by a gentle voice and kind face. There was no sneer of contempt or condescension.

"I'll be fine…,sir," I said, belatedly realizing we'd skipped the accustomed introductions.

"Cooper, Sergeant Cooper, Thames River Police," he said, sparing a glance from the bundle at his feet.

"Sergeant Drummond and this is Constable O'Rourke," I said. "We're here following a possible connection to a woman's murder, a particularly vile case of dismemberment. Due to the size and nature of your find, we'd most appreciate the opportunity to remain."

He looked between us and shrugged.

"Can't promise it won't be grisly, but you both seem of sterner stuff," he said. "Not even sure what it is we 'ave. I might just be overreactin', but my gut is rarely wrong, not when I'm beset with one of me chills."

Flan darted a glance my way and I nodded surreptitiously. While rarer in men, it wasn't unheard of for some, especially sailors and those whose work brings them in tune with the tides, to retain a keen sense of instinct. This man Drummond likely had some minor psychic ability.

"That cloth," I said, leaning in for a closer look at the large bundle. "Is that a woman's dress?"

"Widow's weeds, mum, if I'm not mistaken," he said, mopping his brow. "Black as night, they is. Full mourning these, unless they weren't as dark before the river soaked into 'em."

What was contained inside the black dress was of vital import and yet, I hesitated to pull back the fabric to reveal the foul item beneath. As if sensing this, Flan turned her attention to the water seeping onto the jetty's rough wooden surface.

There was an ominous reddish-brown tinge to the water pooling around the bundle that she inspected closely. She crouched down, dipped a white handkerchief into the befouled liquid, and held it aloft to the oily sunlight.

"Blood?" Sergeant Cooper asked.

"Hard to be sure, especially with the tannins in the water here, but if I had to bet, I'd say yes," she said.

Flan slipped the hanky into an envelope of waxed paper which I was sure she'd pocket when the sergeant wasn't looking.

"If there be no complaints, we ought be about our foul business then," Cooper said, hands clasped before him and eyes downcast. "It is a bleak thing this, if my gut be correct. I'm not sure about you, but I'd rather be done with it quick like."

"Yes, of course, Sergeant," I said. "No need to draw the horrid unveiling out further. These streets, the river included, we vowed to protect. We must be about our work if justice be done."

I took a deep breath and held it firm within my chest, preparing for the worst. But even so prepared, and with Flan's steady presence at my shoulder, I was stricken with horror as Sergeant Cooper gingerly pulled back the sodden, black fabric.

I fought the revulsion that overcame me, the primal urge to flee to safety. But where in all the empire would a woman be safe with such a dark and sinister force at work?

This woman's body had been desecrated in a manner so heinous it was quite beyond the pale. Once again, the head and limbs had been removed with precision, neatly disarticulated by someone with skill and ritualized intention, but beyond these similarities there had been a change in his methods. While the dismemberment was cold and calculating, quite remarkably methodical, the damage to her lower abdomen was evidence of enraged, frenzied hatred.

And there, standing out starkly against her pale, bloated skin were the marks of a magic most evil.

The arcane sigils were at once familiar and nauseating, the bilious effect made all the stronger by the ghostly image of the woman, whole if forlorn, superimposed upon the torso that was all that was left of the violated corpse.

"Good God, miss," Cooper said, lurching away from the body, face ashen. "What foul fiend could do such a thing to a body?"

What foul fiend, indeed.

AMONGST THE VERMIN

Forneus

Chapter 12

Licking my lips in eager anticipation, I used my walking stick to slowly part the folds of the shabby curtain that was all that stood between me and a stranger's delicious secrets. After weeks of wearisome legal tasks most tedious and mundane, one could only hope for a discovery most foul.

The room, nothing more than an alcove really, was filled to bursting with the lowliest of loathsome wretches. Twelve such vermin huddled together, filthy bodies pressed shoulder to shoulder as they bowed to the thirteenth man, the mysterious mutton-chopped gentleman I'd followed past the berths of the opium den. I daresay, my curiosity was piqued.

But it wasn't until the miserable wastrels raised their bowed heads, faces rapt with pleasure, that I became fully aware of my enormous good fortune. The need for secrecy, if not the reason behind the clandestine meeting, was readily apparent.

Rapt adoration wasn't the only thing distorting the men's faces. Muscles contorted to such extremes that the skin at nose and temples were split and festering around wide, gleaming eyes. Drool ran in long, thick strands from the distorted, gaping mouths of men who were no longer alone in their bodies.

No, these twelve men were quite obviously inhabited by slogoth demons, a situation that would ultimately lead to their untimely demise. Until that eventuality, these pitiable creatures appeared to be in service to the gentlemen whose face remained in shadow.

A curious turn of events, indeed.

The gentleman raised his hand, stifling the guttural mutterings and indistinct moans that had poured from the possessed men like wind through tattered sails. The sudden silence was thick with promise. It was all I could do to restrain myself from dancing about the opium den in delight.

How I'd yearned for something, anything to break me free from the quotidian monotony of my immortal existence.

Here was a most engaging puzzle, a meeting of demons that I was quite sure was unauthorized from our lord and master. To what foul purpose, what singularly dark path were they set?

So distracted were the tantalizing possibilities, I nearly missed the gentleman's words as he broke the tomb-like silence.

"Our work progresses," he said, looking to each possessed man in turn. His low, rumbling voice was hypnotic, causing the men to sway.

"Yesss, sssir," the men replied in unison, the words seeping and oozing past broken teeth and tortured souls.

"But we need more power," he said. "There must be more sacrifices if we're to open the gateway."

"Yesss, sssir," the men said.

"And the work of our fallen brothers must be unearthed," he said. "We must shake the very foundations of our former lodge and awaken the bones. Their work will not be in vain. We will complete their work and build a door for our master to walk through once more."

The possessed men moaned and writhed in ecstasy and torment, even as they bowed and exited through a trapdoor hidden beneath a shabby, threadbare piece of carpet. The stench of river filled the room, assaulting my heightened senses.

Here was a plot so devious, I wish I'd hatched it myself. I was as of yet uncertain if I would set my mind to supporting or ruining their plans. For now, the awakening of predatory instincts long buried had an invigorating effect.

I set off in pursuit, eager to learn more of this man and his evil deeds.

MUDLARKS AND NIGHTINGALES

Cora

Chapter 13

Not quite ready to take Flan's advice for a séance, or recovered yet enough to summon the creature Jonathan, I turned to a more mundane, mortal source of information. It required a trip to Commercial Street. I pushed through noisy throngs intent on commerce or the entertainment of public houses, gin palaces, or the many gaming halls that lined both sides of the street. There was much here to remind a soul of what we fight for and how far we yet must come.

It was here on this street of vice, rife with sorrow and criminality lurking beneath the bright sheen of purchased amusement, I knew I'd find Billie Dilwyn Leverton. Billie was a friend, but as they and Flan had run in rival gangs of pickpockets and housebreakers in their youth, I'd sent my constable on an errand. I didn't have the time or patience to deal with the boasting and bickering, no matter how good-natured.

"You're looking well, Billie," I said, thankful for the informality of meeting on the street since I was never too certain of the formal pronoun to use and I hadn't worked up the courage to ask.

There was a sharpness to their cheekbones, a striking feature certainly, but nothing to suggest malnourishment. No, if Billie hungered it was only to see an extra ounce of joy in every soul they encountered. It was a noble goal and one I mightily hoped they achieved.

"And you, Miss Drummond, are radiant as always," Billie said, waving a hand in my direction.

"It's kind of you to notice," I stammered. "I like your new frock."

Some might find Billie's rouge and beard, or dress paired with a gentleman's frock coat incongruous. But Billie embraced their unconventionality in a way that I strongly admired. We don't all fit into convenient boxes. And the pale green Billie wore suited them immensely.

"It's the color of the season," they said, brushing a hand down the voluminous skirts with a flourish.

Billie was a thief gifted at housebreaking and the fabric of their dress was obviously of a rich and fine quality. I turned a blind eye to Billie's less than legal activities in exchange for information. Their criminal network, and extensive and various friends, made Billie a highly valued asset.

"I won't ask where you acquired it," I said.

"Probably for the best," they said with a wink.

I cleared my throat and leaned forward, keeping my voice conspiratorially low.

"Now, have you heard any rumors regarding anything unnatural or whispers about women being murdered, their bodies dumped in the river?" I asked. "Anything at all, no matter how trivial, might help my investigation."

The cheeky grin was gone, replaced by sharp, intelligent eyes that glanced furtively up and down the busy street.

"One of my girls saw a man with dead eyes drag a large parcel out of a hansom cab and dump it in the river," they said.

Billie bit their lip and I knew I had to choose my words with care.

"More women will die if we don't catch this man, Billie," I said. "One of your girls could be next. And the things he and his friends do to the bodies, it bears not repeating."

"But I think you must repeat it, Miss Cora," they said. "For who will look after the women of Whitechapel if we do not? And how must we do so without being forearmed with all that we collectively know?"

"You're right, Billie," I said. "We are stronger together."

"Damn right we are, miss," they said.

So, I proceeded to pretend to shop up and down Commercial Street, with Billie at my elbow, all the while covertly recounting everything I knew so far of the case.

"It's ghastly," Billie said, face drawn and pallid. "I thought I'd heard and seen the worst of these streets, but the way this monster breaks these women down into their parts, like pieces of a macabre puzzle, and the grisly desecration of their flesh, this is the worst of what men can do. I am sick with it."

Something in what Billie said regarding the women as puzzle pieces, pawns in a twisted game, resonated within me and I filed the idea away for later. Perhaps my team could make sense of it once we had the archive files in hand. For now, I waited, sensing that Billie had more to share.

"It seems evident that whoever has done this thing, the person committing such heinous, unspeakable acts, has a great disregard for members of the fairer sex," they said.

"Indeed, he vents his rage upon these women during or soon after the murder," I said with a nod. "It's likely he hates women, or at least hates those who are not men."

"The evidence also points to a wicked skill with the blade and at least rudimentary knowledge of anatomy," they said. "The way he methodically dismembers the bodies can't be the result of luck or accident."

"Quite so," I said.

I'd been pondering the same, but it helped to hear the idea said aloud. It was troubling to think of a man of medical science, a man who'd sworn an oath to protect and heal, being capable of such horrors. But I had to remind myself that we may be dealing with more than a mere man. With the evidence of demonic interference in the nearby Flower and Dean rookery, it was plausible that any man committing such acts might be doing so under hellish influence or at the mercy of a sinister cabal.

A chill ran up my spine and it had little to do with the dead woman who appeared over Billie's shoulder.

"Have any girls gone missing that you know of?" I asked.

Billie started to shake their head, but halted abruptly, face going a sickly green.

"Rose Thornberry," they said. "Singer at the music hall here on Commercial Street. Rose is her stage name, of course. Don't know her given name."

"Then I think I should drop by the music hall for a visit," I said.

I would collect Flan and investigate this girl Rose's disappearance. I prayed that the singer was deep in her cups somewhere or run off with a lad. Anything would be preferable to death at the hands of the torso murderer.

Anything at all.

Chapter 14

The manager at the music hall was of little help and so it was, armed only with a playbill with the missing woman's likeness, that Flan and I descended to a muddy stretch of the Thames where men, women, and children searched for treasures amidst the foul-smelling detritus.

Flan, recognizing one of the young women scavenging closer to the river, put two fingers in her mouth and whistled. The girl, a child really, looked up and gave Flan a small wave before going back to her labors.

"It's a hard life," I said, troubled. "We shouldn't disturb her unduly."

I reached up for Flan's hand as she made to whistle again. We both froze, eyes locked, as my fingers brushed her lips. Suddenly, there were no demons, no foul murders, no impoverished mudlarks, or the smell of river rot.

There was only me and Flan.

She grinned and I blushed so fiercely, I thought I might faint, which was absolutely ridiculous.

"Are you alright?" Flan asked, stepping closer, grin replaced by a frown of concern, the fingers that had been between her lips now reaching out to steady me.

My God, why did I have to keep thinking about her lips?

"I'm fine," I said. "Just overwarm."

My eyes slid once again to her lips and I knew then that I was well and truly ensnared. Flan had made clear her intentions, but I had dissembled, claiming that I was worried about how our growing relationship would affect our work, though truth to tell I was worried about more than a power dynamic that Flan refused to recognize.

She'd made it clear more than once that she believed we were equals in all things. She followed my orders because she trusted me, not because of an established hierarchy within special branch. No, I was worried about more than our difference in rank.

I was frightened of what would happen if I gave away my heart. What I hadn't realized until now was that the organ was already given.

I ducked behind a snail encrusted wooden pile and a stack of broken crates.

"Are you ill?" Flan asked, following close at my heels. "If you've had too much sun, there are better places to find shade..."

I spun and pulled her to me, stopping her words with a kiss.

Oh, what a kiss.

Maybe, I really had received too much sun. For surely, I was beset with fever. My skin burned everywhere that Flan and I touched, and as she reached her hand to cup the back of my neck, I trembled.

It was only the cry of a gull that broke the spell, a reminder that the eyes of strangers were close by. With a shaky breath, we parted, resting forehead to forehead as we regained ourselves.

"My God, Cora," Flan said. "I never thought that would happen again."

"Are you glad it did?" I asked, straightening and casting a covert glance up through my lashes.

"Do you really need to ask?" she asked, eyebrows disappearing beneath her cap.

Warmth swelled my chest as certainty filled me.

"We fit together like the finest gloves, always have," I said with a smile.

"Always will, if that kiss means you accept my declaration," she said, removing her hat.

She looked vulnerable, and so I did what I could to reassure her.

Chapter 15

The sun had shifted and most of the mudlarks were gone when we ventured from behind the crates. But the girl we'd seen before was still nearby, bent over a piece of oil cloth piled with her day's work. Broken pottery and a rusted tin sat side by side with a lovely earing and a tangle of netting. It was the item trapped inside the net, and the ghost that hovered above it, that was the current source of my disquiet.

"The net," I croaked, swallowing hard. "There's a body there."

The girl was inspecting the earring now, holding it close to her face. She wore wire-rimmed spectacles, but one lens was cracked and the other was missing entirely.

"Give me a shilling," Flan whispered.

"Why?" I asked, distracted by the dead girl dripping river water onto the tangle of rope.

"So, I can buy her day's haul and send her away none the wiser that she's found a mutilated corpse," she said.

"Oh, yes, of course," I said.

Flan took the coin and proceeded to haggle with the girl. The child made a good show of being unwilling to part with her treasures, but she couldn't hide the satisfied smile as she slipped the money, and the earring, into her pocket and scarpered up the muddy beach. We waited for the girl to ascend the rickety stairs to the street above before Flan began cutting at the ropes with one of the many knives she kept about her person.

This murderer, this vile defiler of women, was an evil creature.

"Is it her?" Flan asked, removing the last of the rope.

I didn't need to examine the playbill in my pocket, or the ghost hovering nearby, to know that the torso at my feet belonged to the missing girl from the music hall. There was a distinct, memorable birthmark just below her collarbone, unmolested by the many arcane sigils carved deep into her flesh, in the shape of a rose.

Our quarry, a murderer most devious, had done his foul butchery once more.

GAME OF SHADOWS

Forneus

Chapter 16

The trapdoor led to a series of tunnels and underground passageways lit here and there with torchlight. The stench of decay hung heavy on torpid air, damp walls glistening with an amphibian gleam.

The demon-possessed men scurried away, hastily dispersing in pursuit of their heinous duties. Rather than following one of these lowly servants, I remained a lithesome shadow dogging the heels of a more promising quarry.

The mysterious gentleman hastened through the tunnels, pausing only to consult a map at one of the many unmarked crossroads. We continued traipsing through the bowels of London for many hours before emerging into the thin, grimy sunlight of dawn.

We'd traveled in a peculiar geometric pattern that had been at once intriguing and disorienting. So it was that my eyes searched out the street sign affixed to a brick building at the first intersection we came to. That is how I knew precisely where my quarry led me as he turned and strode confidently up Craven Street.

Humming and holding an object up to the light of the nearest gas lamp, I could tell the man was quite pleased even though much of his face remained ensconced in shadow. I hastened forward, leaping for a handhold with which to pull myself to a more advantageous position atop a neighboring balcony. It was from this perch that I caught sight of the object in his hand.

What the devil was he doing with a lady's earring? I didn't have time to ponder the question, since he was once again on the move. With the ease and stealth of a spider, I climbed down in pursuit.

Bouncing the earring happily in the palm of his hand, the man halted in front of a building with an architectural peculiarity that made my stomach queasy. A matching unease crept up my spine. I held my breath, tingling with a mixture of anxiety and anticipation.

How long had it been since I'd felt threatened by anything on this beleaguered earthly plane? But I couldn't ignore the alarm bells ringing from centuries of terror in the pit. One misstep would lead to certain doom.

It was positively delightful.

The man reluctantly pocketed the earring and lifted his hand, moving his fingers in a series of arcane gestures. Glinting with an inner fire, the golden ring he wore seemed to draw spectral shapes in the morning air. With a flash, a symbol carved above the door lit with an answering glow.

To my surprise, the entire building began to shake, rumbling and growling like a caged beast. A crevice began to snake its way up the front of the building, a great fissure splitting the glowing symbol with a thunderous crack.

Lightning struck nearby, and the man strode away. I blinked furiously and spun on my heel to follow. It was only later, as I continued to blink away the afterimage, that I recognized the symbol above the door.

The building at 36 Craven Street bore a carving of an architect's square and compass, a secret Masonic symbol. But to what purpose? It was in the untangling of this mystery that my fascination was now firmly rooted.

THE WAR AGAINST EVIL

Cora

Chapter 17

After a day spent slogging through the muck and mire, my unruly workmates were a welcome sight. Even prissy Edith St. Germaine and the tepid tea she thrust at me like a saber were a needed boon of normalcy and warmth after a night and day spent running from demons and enduring the chill of the dead.

"Look at this," Lottie said, pushing a newspaper across the conference table.

"The Times?" I asked, lifting an eyebrow.

Now that I was back in our offices, I'd expected files from the archives, perhaps even a coroner's report, not the evening paper.

"Just because the boys at the Yard haven't reported it, doesn't mean there's nothing suspicious afoot," Flan said, dropping into a chair and lighting a cigarette.

Lottie and Flan were right. It wouldn't be the first time our "silly little circle" found a pattern in the city's newspapers.

I skimmed the headlines, looking for anything suspicious. One article in particular caught my eye.

According to the article, archaeologists from the British Museum's department of antiquities were to be brought in after numerous human and animal remains were unearthed today at a prominent Craven Street address. The grisly discovery was made as workers were inspecting the basement and foundation after neighbors complained of late-night building tremors. During the peculiarly focused earthquake, cracks and fissures appeared across the building's façade and along support structures. The cause of the tremors, and subsequent damage, is unknown, but some citizens have voiced concern over recent ambitious feats of engineering in the construction of the nearby Victoria Embankment. Spokesmen for the Royal Corps of Engineers have refused to comment.

"Numerous human and animal remains does sound promising," I said, tentatively reaching out and tapping the newspaper article.

"If a heap of bones and witching hour building tremors aren't a case, I'll eat my hat," Flan said, pinching the ember from her cigarette and putting the remaining inch of rolled tobacco behind her ear.

"I wish you would," Edith said, wrinkling her nose. "That thing smells horrid and doesn't befit a lady."

Flan rolled to her feet and cracked her knuckles, but Lottie loomed between them. I scowled, massaging my temples, and Anna came to my rescue.

"Miss Lottie always says to start a day with a hearty breakfast," she said, sliding a plate of scones onto the table. "But I think you've all been too busy to eat."

"I'm not hungry," Flan said with a scowl, frowning at Edith, but her stomach let out a mighty growl.

"Liar," Edith said with a smirk.

"I don't think we need your psychic gift to tell if that's a lie or not, Edith," I said with a grin. "Come on, Anna's right. We've all been hard at it. Let's have tea while you give your reports. I'm eager to learn more about those symbols carved into the women's bodies, and if we have anything helpful from the archives."

"I took care of the exorcism, in case anyone cares," Edith said, sniffing irritably.

"Of course, we care, Miss Edith," Anna said. "Those poor people."

Lottie patted little Anna's arm consolingly, and even Edith softened.

"Not to worry, Anna," Edith said. "Their bodies and their souls remain their own to do with as they will. Now the wellbeing of the men and women of the Flower and Dean rookery is between each of them and God."

"Thank you, Edith," I said. "I never doubted your thoroughness. I hope the priest will keep the situation in confidence?"

"There is no doubt," she said with a curt nod.

If Edith St. Germaine put the question to the man and he said he would keep our secret, then I didn't doubt the veracity of her claim.

"So, where are we with the archival records?" I asked. "Anything on the arcane sigils, or the Barnes case?"

"I…," Anna stammered, blushing, eyes focused on her lap.

"Yes, Constable Russell?" I asked.

Flan raised an eyebrow at me, but I shrugged. Perhaps, reminding the young woman of her rank would help her find her tongue. Anna jerked her head back, thrust out her chin, and placed her hands on the table.

"I believe that Kate Webster, the maid who killed and dismembered Julia Martha Thomas, was possessed by a demon," Anna said. Her voice shook, but more now from a passion for justice than from nerves. "And it's not just the manner in which she butchered that poor woman. As you know, when a person dies in prison or the workhouses and nobody pays to claim them for burial, the body is given to science. But after Kate Webster was hanged at Wandsworth Prison, no body ever made it to the anatomy school it was bound for. There was a complaint of only receiving a container of liquified remains, boneless and long spoiled."

"Like what's left after possession by a slogoth demon," Flan said, frowning. "Eventually, the human body dissolves, liquifies as if by a powerful acid, and the diminutive demon emerges. That's not what you encountered in the rookery."

"No," I said, shaking my head.

"Definitely not," Edith said. "If it'd been slogoth demons, there'd have been no saving those people."

"Any other reason to believe Kate Webster was a demon?" I asked.

"Well, just look at her!" Anna said, pushing a photograph across the table.

A chill ran along my spine, and I stifled a shiver. There was something unnatural in the pose, more similar to death photography than an image of the living, and yet there was vitality, or at least a strong force, looking out through wide eyes.

Even more chilling was the shadowy figure in the background. The man's face was blurry and indistinct, but he dressed like a man of means and he had large, mutton-chop whiskers. Over his shoulder hung a mirror that held a vague man-like shape, likely a reflection of the man from behind.

"Good work, constable," I said, swallowing hard. "And the arcane markings on the body?"

"They match the ones on our victims," Lottie said.

"So, we have dismembered bodies of women, carved with arcane sigils, going back at least a year," I said.

"It gets worse," Lottie said. "Those markings? According to the archives, those markings are a combination of Masonic symbolism, black magic, necromancy, and demonic summoning rituals."

"Bloody hell," Flan swore.

Not even Edith reprimanded Flan for her foul tongue. We were all too shocked by the implications. The mass possession in the rookery hadn't been the beginning. It was a symptom, a byproduct of the rituals of these murders.

Someone, or something, was directing the murders of multiple women and the desecration of their bodies as part of a dark magic ritual. Unlike the men who murder for profit or in a moment of passion, I knew our killer wouldn't stop killing until his ritual was complete, or we brought him justice.

"We are soldiers in the war against evil," I said, meeting the eye of every member of my team. "We must stop this man, and any dark forces he commands, before another innocent comes to harm."

Chapter 18

We stood outside 36 Craven Street armed with historical data from the S.P.R.B. archives. This had once been the home of Benjamin Franklin, an influential figure believed to be a Freemason, a fact that coincided with the Masonic symbol engraved above the door. At the time that Franklin was in residence, the proprietor's son-in-law, William Hewson, operated an illegal anatomy school in the building's basement.

It was to this basement that we were directed upon calling at the door and showing our warrant cards. The men from the British Museum had not yet arrived to examine the bones and I hoped to conclude our search before we fell under their scrutiny.

The footman at least had no desire to linger. As soon as his footsteps receded up the stairs, I turned my attention to the bones, though "bones" does not convey the magnitude of what lay before us.

"Good god," I muttered.

"Mother Mary in heaven," Lottie said.

Edith crossed herself and Anna huddled close to Lottie's side.

"It's a mass grave," Flan said. "The poor souls are mixed together; men, women, children, and animals."

However these people had died, their bones had been cruelly used. The bones were carved with the same arcane markings that had become all too familiar in the hunt for our killer.

In addition to this vile denigration and blasphemy, the human and animal remains were laid together in a strange geometrical pattern and sealed within the building's foundation.

"And not in consecrated ground," Edith said, aghast.

"Far from, I'd say," I said, leaning forward.

The same earthquake that unearthed the Craven Street bones had damaged the mortar, but a terrible story lurked beyond the spiderweb of cracks and fissures.

"Flan, bring me that lamp," I said, squinting at the wall's textured surface.

"What is it, Miss Cora?" Anna whispered.

I brushed gloved fingers along the stone and mortar, feeling for a recognizable symbol or character. There was a pattern here, I was sure of it.

Flan brought us the lamp and Edith hissed. I flinched away from the wall as if burned. The stone, and its carving of dancing shadows, told a dreadful tale of torment, sacrifice, and rebirth.

"Good heavens!" Lottie blurted, pulling Anna closer as if to shield the young woman from this evil, for there was no doubt that this was indeed the blackest of plans.

"The serpent," Flan said, moving close enough to brush my shoulder. "Is that the Thames?"

The hair lifted along my neck and it had little to do with Flan's breath at my ear. Billie had commented on how this man broke women down into their parts, as if they were pieces to a puzzle, or pawns in a game. This occult map revealed the dreadful truth of the matter, proving that our friend was quite correct in their perceptions.

"The serpent symbolizes rebirth, transformation, and immortality," Edith said with a frown.

"And we're in a Masonic lodge," Flan said. "Making these the blueprints for a secret brotherhood of architects."

"Does that mean we face more than one foe, Miss Cora?" Lottie asked, a tightening around the eyes revealing the degree of her concern. "We did wonder as much with the number of men and women possessed in the rookery. But this..."

"This is grotesque," Edith said. "This is an abomination."

"I do believe these are blueprints," I said. I nodded, choosing my words carefully. "The toolmarks on the bones, the dismemberment of the bodies, the carved torsos in the Thames, and, according to this map, the precise placement of the limbs and skulls throughout London, all point to one thing. Whether we face one man or many, what is happening in our city has been planned carefully and the machinations and implementation of it began more than a century ago."

"To what end, Miss Cora?" Anna asked.

"The river is the key," Lottie said, pointing to the wall.

“They use the disassembled parts to direct power to the river, and they feed the river the largest portion, sacrificing to the serpent as a magical means to give birth,” I said.

“But give birth to what?” Anna asked.

“To a great evil.”

AN INPENETRABLE MYSTERY

Forneus

Chapter 19

What had begun as a hunter stalking its prey had sadly become a case of trudging tediously through London's grey and grimy streets. It was all so dreadfully monochrome and monotonous. The incessant fog and drizzle seeped into my clothing, no matter how many times I used my magic to burn away the damp, and I daresay I now smelled of horses.

I scowled, wishing there was someone I could smite. I grew weary of this hunt. Only the promise of discovering a dark secret kept me in pursuit.

I was considering my regrettable decision not to follow one of this man's demonic minions, when the gentleman turned sideways and disappeared. Now that was interesting. I raised an eyebrow and hastened to where I'd last seen the man.

A quick inspection of the brick wall revealed nothing. It was only after tapping the bricks with my cane that the truth became apparent. I pressed two of the bricks with gloved fingers and a large portion of wall spun silently on a hinge. The opening was narrow, just large enough for a man, or demon, to disappear into the darkness within.

I slipped inside, a grin tugging at my lips. I followed the sound of strangled screams through a dark, covered courtyard and up a narrow flight of stairs. The smile fell from my lips as I peered into the room beyond.

The lodgings were small, but the furniture had been pushed to the side and stacked along one wall. On the floor of the cramped room, a chalk circle was drawn and marked with unholy symbols that now glowed with a painful, searing light. Within the circle huddled two mewling slogoth demons.

"Pleassse, massster," they cried. "Let uss ssserve!"

But the gentleman was displeased, his ire apparent in the quivering of his whiskers. These lowly creatures had made a tragic misstep, at their master's orders I am sure, and were to face the consequences of their failure.

With a forceful hand motion, the bones of the demons broke. A second flick of the man's wrist, and the light of the circle increased in intensity, and the demons exploded.

I could barely contain my anger. We demons are often the scapegoat for man's failures and disgrace. But to punish so cruelly these poor slogoth demons, little more than the golden retrievers of Hell, was unconscionable.

I would discover this man's secret, of that I was certain, and then I would make him pay.

TABLE-KNOCKING MISADVENTURE

Cora

Chapter 20

For over a hundred years, these tortured souls had been denied a proper burial and their eternal rest. Our next move was clear to me, albeit unwelcome.

The ghosts had, until now, been silent as the grave. But there was a distinct scratching in the walls and along the floorboards that I did not believe to be rats. The dead were restless.

It was time.

"Gather your things," I said. "We're holding a séance this evening at our Whitechapel lodgings."

It was most peculiar for a Spiritualist society, as the public considered us to be, to take up residence in Whitechapel. Séances were more common in the parlors of the peerage than in the squalor of the East End, but if that gave us an added air of eccentricity, that suited our purposes well.

While Agnes lived, we'd given dramatic readings, sometimes as a method for gathering intelligence, sometimes to give a local woman a bit of potentially life-saving advice, and, in Agnes' case, a way to communicate with the spirit realm. Her guides had often imparted tidbits of information that assisted us in our work. But I wasn't a clairvoyant, and I had no practical training as a medium.

All I knew was that the dead women haunted me, and I would do anything to prevent others from their tragic fate.

Chapter 21

I slowed my breathing and tried not to fidget with my shawl as Edith and Anna finished drawing the curtains. Lottie replaced the candle in the center of the table with a fresh taper in a silver holder and fussed over the multitude of oddments set on the table's lace cloth.

Flan looked ready for battle. She paced the room, glaring into shadowed corners as if daring the dead women to appear. I sipped my tea, a blend Agnes swore helped to cleanse and prepare the body before a séance, trying to soothe a throat gone dry and tight.

I hated this. I shifted in the hard, wooden chair, grateful only that we were holding this séance in private. When Agnes had opened the doors to the public, we'd often locked her inside a spirit cabinet to prove the legitimacy of her psychic talents.

The very thought of being so constrained forced the air from my lungs and made my skin itch. How had she managed to tolerate such confinement? If my dearly departed constable ever reached out to me from the spiritual plane, I had a great deal of apologizing to do.

I jumped in my seat, startled as a hand settled on my shoulder.

"We're ready," Flan said with an apologetic smile.

She took her seat beside me and, as we all joined hands, Flan gave my fingers a reassuring squeeze. My cheeks warmed and I flashed her a grateful smile. While I'm sure the smile didn't reach my eyes, I was thankful for Flan's steady presence at my side.

Indeed, I was grateful for my entire team. We'd all felt the profound loss of our teammate deeply, and to be here in a space so completely hers was a singular kind of agony. Agnes was a casualty of this war, even before we'd known the full breadth of our enemy's plan.

I would not let her sacrifice be in vain.

Staring into the middle distance, I allowed my focus to soften, blurring the candle's flame into a fuzzy orb that appeared to float above the table's surface. The faces of my constables became indistinct, more pale orbs floating, as if disembodied, in the smoke-filled air.

Someone had lit the bowl of sage and I drew the acrid smoke through my nostrils, hoping to purify my body and ready it for whatever was to come. I hesitated, sensing the room fill with ghostly apparitions, but eventually I had to open my eyes, including my third eye, and see the spirits of the dead.

I nearly swooned, so dizzying was the press of cold bodies. Dozens of women hovered along the walls as if hung from the pressed tin ceiling, dripping river water upon the parlor floor. I did, however, shiver as a chill breeze stirred, lifting my hair, and I knew with certainty that a great many women floated behind my chair.

I reached out before me, avoiding a glance over my shoulder, to lift the silver bell that would help give voice to these women. For though it terrified me, I would give the dead an opportunity to name their killer and bring judgement upon him.

But as my fingertips touched the frosted surface of the bell, the ghosts fled our parlor and the walls ran red with blood.

"You rang?"

A man stepped from the shadows, a smug smile upon cruel lips. I reached for the revolver I kept pocketed in my skirts, but my movements were sluggish, the chill of the dead set deeply into my bones.

Flan was not so afflicted. She jumped to her feet, brandishing a wicked blade and quite prepared to use it.

"Sweet Mother Mary who art in heaven," Edith said, making the sign of the cross. "He's a demon."

"Are such hysterics necessary?" he said, waving a hand theatrically, hiding the wince Edith's prayer had inflicted.

"Tell us your purpose, demon, and your name," I said. "And know that my constable has the ability to recognize the truth when she hears it. Lie to us and we will send you straight back to the pit."

"Come now, I do like to make an entrance, but appearing during your séance was just a bit of fun," Forneus said, waving away sage smoke with a lace-trimmed handkerchief. "And, for the record, I'm not the one who ruined the wallpaper."

"Your name, demon," I said.

"Fine, fine," he said with a sigh. "I am the demon lord, Forneus, Grand Marquis of Hell, blah, blah, blah. I do believe we are short on time. Must I recite my many titles?"

"Why are you here, *Forneus*," I said.

There was a power in a name. Judging from the demon's frown and Edith's nod, he'd given us his true name. A small degree of tension loosened from my shoulders, but I held my revolver tightly. It wouldn't do to trust a demon.

"You do want to know where to find the man going around killing the women of Whitechapel, don't you?" he said.

"And why would you side with us?" I asked, holding his attention.

Flan had circled the table, creeping up behind Forneus. If the demon so much as twitched, she'd gut him from stem to stern.

"Because the man you're looking for, the one who goes by the name of Sir Thomas Goswick, has no imagination," he said, sniffing disdainfully. "I grow tiresome of his plodding methods. Plus, he's no friend to my kind. I do draw that line at torturing puppies, so to speak."

Another small bit of tension left me. Until now, I'd worried that our murderer might be none other than Lysander Snidely-Moore. Though the inspector was odious, it would have been a harsh blow if the S.P.R.B. had been infiltrated by such a fiend.

"I don't believe him," Flan said. "Isn't our enemy summoning a creature from Hell? And has demonic minions? Sounds like he likes hellspawn just fine."

"He's telling the truth," Edith said with a grimace. "Much as I hate to say it. The demon hasn't lied, yet."

"Too right," Forneus said with a smile. "This Goswick fellow must be stopped. He summons, enslaves, and tortures lower demons, not really friendly behavior."

"And the purpose of his work?" I asked. "Murdering and sacrificing the women whose spirits so recently occupied this very room?"

"Goswick attempts to open a door to another realm," he said, fire flickering behind his eyes. "As for the creature he's trying to summon, I don't know who or what it is, but that gateway doesn't lead to Hell. Of that I am certain."

UNLIKELIEST OF ALLIES

Cora

Chapter 22

"If you despise this Sir Thomas Goswick and his methods, why don't you stop him?" I asked, eyes narrowing at the demon. "Why come to us?"

"Because he matters little to me," Forneus said. "And because I am not yet ready to draw the attention of my lord and master. Not for a tedious toad such as Goswick."

"But you'll tell us where we can find the man," Flan said.

"Of course," he said. "What you do with that information is up to you. Though, of course, I do hope that whatever course of action you take will be entertaining. Ah, yes. That would truly be splendid."

Forneus gave us the address as promised, and I shook my head. Of course, our investigation would lead us back to the Flower and Dean rookery. There was a symmetry to that revelation that made perfect sense.

After another quarter hour of condescending pedantry, the demon took his leave. But I was certain he dogged our heels as we sped down narrow alleys and side streets, the passageways here faster on foot than by carriage.

The demon wasn't the only creature flitting through the shadows in our wake. Ghostly apparitions and the stench of rot and river water were never far behind. So, it was with extreme effort that I stared straight ahead as I flagged down the nearest policeman, showed him my warrant card, and handed him a letter.

"Send this telegram here," I said, thrusting the instructions at the young man. "It is a matter of urgency. The very security of the empire may depend upon it."

The young man blanched, but tipped his helmet and with a hasty "yes, m'am" ran as he was ordered.

"Reinforcements?" Flan asked.

"I've put in a request, but whether or not they deem to send us more men, or even if they reach us in time, is yet to be seen," I said.

We renewed our speed and the street filled with a chill wind. Somewhere a clock struck the hour, the tolling of the bells matched by my heart thundering in my chest. I was nearly knocked off my feet, carried by a grim tide, as the spirits of the dead pressed in from all sides. There was an urgency to the dead women, a frenzy to their movements that filled me with terror. Their message was clear.

We were running out of time.

Chapter 23

Painfully out of breath, we fanned out in front of Wilmott's Lodging House. Thrawl Street was unnaturally silent, as if the entire rookery held its collective breath. Not even a babe dare cry on this night.

"Come, let us find this Goswick and bring an end to this foul business," I said.

My teammates smiled grimly but followed me inside the warren of rooms and passageways. The walls began to weep, and a chill breeze tugged at my ankles, pulling me toward a flight of stairs at the back of the building.

"Where are the lodgers?" Edith asked. "This place was filled to the brim not a day ago."

"Up," I said, a strange resonance to my voice, as if my vocal cords were a violin's strings being dragged painfully with a bow. "The roof."

Flan flashed a questioning look my way, but I had no explanation to give. I was caught in a chill tide, and no matter how I dreaded it, the spirits of the dead flowed through me now. If they said Goswick was on the roof, then up the stairs we'd go.

With limbs gone stiff with the cold, I ran. I'm not even sure how I managed to retain my dagger, the chill took me so. And so it was, with frost riming my eyelids, and my breath fogging on a mild summer night, we burst onto the rooftops of the Flower and Dean rookery to face an agent for darkness.

Sir Thomas Goswick moved jerkily as if tugged at by a puppeteer, but the dog-sized demons at his feet fanned out to face us. Though small in stature, these demons sported deadly fangs that glistened with venom. The venom was a reminder that these demons recently inhabited the bodies of human men, until the acid liquified their remains.

I reached into my pocket and swallowed hard. We must take down Goswick, no matter what.

Forneus stepped from the shadows, and I gripped my blade tighter. But he wasn't here to thwart us. Indeed, he was no hindrance at all. He crouched before the slogoth demons, and in one fell swoop eliminated our foes.

"Come here, little ones," Forneus said, scooping the diminutive demons into his arms and cooing to them. "You are safe now. Uncle Forneus won't let anyone harm you."

The slimy, little critters mewled and cried, and for once I was glad that Forneus was on their side. We all need a champion, someone who sees past our flaws to the goodness within. For me, that person was Flan and she was in the thick of it now. Dear God, let her survive this chaos.

With the demons gone from this fight, we now faced the wrath of Sir Thomas Goswick. It was readily apparent, from the wild gleam in his eye to the froth of spittle at his lips, that this man had become unhinged.

I'd seen such frenzied rage before, the day that a man struck down Agnes and removed a beautiful light from this world. Armed with a righteous fire in my belly, I strode forward, dagger in hand. But a force like a freight train hit my shoulder, knocking me from my feet, as a crack of thunder shook the rooftop.

"Cora, oh god, Cora," Flan said, sliding to the ground, my head against her chest.

I blinked, a searing pain in my arm and something warm and wet blurring my vision.

Lottie and Edith jumped onto Goswick and a man's boot knocked a revolver from the man's hand. Another man barked orders—was that Snidely-Moore's voice—and the roof filled with the pounding feet of reinforcements.

I caught glimpses of the sky, a stained ceiling spotted with rings of mold, and heard the whinnies of a horse. A black Mariah stood on the street, and the peculiarly corpse-like face of Sir Thomas Goswick stared out through the bars. We finally had our man and he would soon see justice, of that I was certain.

For a second, I caught sight of Forneus and felt him press a note into my hand. Flan murmured that we were okay, that our team, though bloodied, had survived. Then everything went black.

Chapter 24

"We won," I said, a brisk wind stealing the words from my lips.

The evening's rain had washed the streets of London, banishing the ever-present fog that held the East End captive in its suffocating embrace. The view from atop the Tower regaled with man's greatest accomplishments, while the very tower stones were seeped with centuries of blood.

I shouldn't have been surprised that the demon had wanted to meet here of all places.

"At what cost?" Forneus said, his reply coming from the shadows at my left shoulder.

Neither his ability to read my thoughts nor his stealthy appearance came as a surprise. The demon had an unsettling knack for cutting to the bone of truth, a flagrant disregard for propriety, and an obvious delight for sinister symbolism.

"I am familiar with the origins of the word sinister," I said, eyes never leaving the twinkling dreamscape of flickering gas lamps below. "Though standing at my left shoulder is indulgently redundant, even for you."

"You haven't answered my question," he said.

I took a deep, steadying breath as dizziness washed over me. The sensation had more to do with the demon's words than with the creaking scaffolding beneath my feet. Just as was the case with the city below, sections of this great structure were in disrepair. But that was not what now burdened my thoughts.

The truth was that the cost to bring the Thames torso killer to justice had indeed been high. Our team had suffered losses. My injuries would slow me down considerably and threatened my ability to lead our unit in the field. But physical injury might be the least of our worries.

We were once again reduced in the eyes of our male compatriots within the S.P.R.B., earning their ire rather than respect with the receipt of the Queen's thanks. Working alongside a demon had only deepened their suspicions that women, especially women with psychic gifts, were inherently weak, evil, and not to be trusted.

"Does the individual cost matter if we win the battle?" I asked

"Not if it loses you the war," he said. "Have you considered that your sacrifices might just be a part of your enemy's grand design, another strategic move on the gameboard?"

And that, I daresay, was the rub. Forneus' mutterings might well be improbable lunacy, but I'd be remiss not to consider the possibility that the killer and his demon summoning cabal were not working alone. Indeed, I'd poured over the evidence these past few days and come to a similar conclusion.

"It's unlikely that our killer had the intellect necessary to plan and execute the murders with such precision, even with the aid of his demonic minions," I said. I lifted my chin, ignoring the growing disquiet that came with giving voice to the conviction that we'd been deftly played. "While Scotland Yard believe we've got our man, and Special Branch are convinced we've stamped out the murderous cabal, we're lulled into a false sense of safety, assured in our conviction that men of science will always reign over the supernatural and that good must conquer evil."

"I do believe you're getting warmer," he said.

"Not encouraging words coming from a demon," I said with a wry grin.

"Encouragement has never been my forte, not unless you count encouraging corrupted men to sign over their souls," he said, hungry flame flickering behind his eyes. "I am very, very good at my job."

"I thought you were an attorney to the fae," I said, frowning.

"Never trust 'other duties as assigned' in a job contract," he said ruefully.

I bit my lip, stifling a laugh. But the effort was futile. The anxiety and fear of recent weeks bubbled up in a peal of undignified laughter that had me shaking my head and wiping tears from my cheeks.

A gloved finger touched my face, and I froze. Forneus had moved with a terrifying, alien speed. His touch at once reminding me that I was teetering on a precipice, alone with an inhuman creature with the power to crush me to a bloody pulp, toss me like a ragdoll to the unwitting streets below, or carry me to the burning pits of Hell. The realization was sobering.

"You humans are confounding," he said, tilting his head to examine me with open curiosity.

I was reminded of the view of the operating theater, a body at the mercy of the surgeon's whim. The sense of vulnerability was at once familiar and nauseating. So too was the fear that Forneus might have developed an unhealthy attachment that went beyond our professional agreement.

"Hope, laughter, fear," he muttered. He lifted the hand from my cheek and licked his finger. "Bittersweet."

I struggled to speak, to say something, anything to break the hold of his gaze.

"N-n-no offense, but I don't like men," I said.

"You may have noticed, my dear," he said with a wink. "But I am not a man."

"Or demons!" I blurted, eyes wide.

He howled with laughter and I stumbled back a step, nearly tumbling off the scaffolding. His cane whipped out with lightning speed, halting my descent.

"You misunderstand me," he said. "As highly entertaining and stimulating as our brief correspondence has been, a requisite oasis amidst the barren waste of the tedium of immortality, I do not fancy you," he said. He frowned, tilting his head. "I can't say I have ever fancied a human. Curious that."

Before he decided to sate that curiosity in any possible form, I changed the course of our conversation back to a much safer topic, the devious mastermind behind a series of ritualistic murders.

"If you're correct and there is a grand design to the murders, that would imply a genius mind behind the killings," I said.

"Indubitably," he said, eyes gleaming with a different kind of interest.

"The ability to know the inner workings, or even the existence, of the Special Paranormal Research Branch would require a position of the highest order," I said, shaking my head.

"They wouldn't be the first fiend to climb ranks, or the first good man to become corrupted by power," he said. "Indeed, the privileged often possess the blackest of souls. I am intimately familiar with that constant, immutable truth."

"But is one man, even a man of the most wealthy genteel class, capable of orchestrating such a dreadful string of murders?" I asked.

I bit my lip, ruminating over the brutality of the killings, the surgical precision of the amputations, the artistry of the arcane sigils, and the strategic placement of the bodies all whilst avoiding detection. Nay, whilst leading Scotland Yard and the S.P.R.B. around by our collective noses.

"You know Sir Thomas Goswick was incapable of planning the murders," he said. "You suspected as much as soon as you discovered the man was barely literate, to his family's great shame."

"How on earth do you know that?" I asked. "I only recently read Goswick's file while recovering from my wounds."

In fact, Flan had read the man's file to me along with our case report, since the blood loss from the gunshot wound to my shoulder and the bump to my head had left me too dizzy to read. The ghosts of the dead women, at least, had left me alone, so I knew the lightheadedness to be of natural causes. That thought was less comforting now that I suspected Forneus had been lurking in the corners in their stead.

"I have my ways," he said, splaying long-fingered hands wide.

"If our killer was only a pawn, who is actually playing, and what is his endgame?" I asked.

"Your theory of a sinister cabal is of course accurate, if unambitiously uninspired," he said. "You must expand your theory unfettered by the scope of your jurisdiction."

I looked out past the flickering lights of Whitechapel, to the city of London, and to the world beyond. I imagined the lights being winked out, one by one, across the entire globe, swallowed by a ravenous darkness.

"They did want to open a gateway," I said, a chill running up my spine.

"Yes," he said, nodding. "I do believe that is the goal of our genius puppet master. He's tugging strings here and spinning there, like a spider at the center of a deadly web. And,

I daresay, he has a brotherhood of likeminded minions ready to do his bidding and act out his wishes."

"What's on the other side, trying to break into our world?" I asked.

"Something old, likely hungry, most definitely bored," he said with a shrug.

We were up against a dark fraternity hellbent on opening a gateway to unleash something truly nightmarish on the citizens of London. The world itself might be at stake.

"Will you stay and fight?" I asked.

It was unlikely, even more unlikely than a demon ally, but I had to ask. Forneus was formidable when he put his mind to it.

"Sadly, I have other business to attend," he said with a sigh. "A pity. I would have enjoyed partaking in matching wits against a criminal mastermind, or helping darkness gain dominion over humans, but a demon's work is never done."

I shivered, his words an unsettling reminder that Forneus cared little about the fate of mere humans. Now more than ever, I'd need to rely on my team. Our numbers were small, and we lacked the support of our comrades within the S.P.R.B., but together we just might succeed.

Together, we would remain vigilant against the rising tide of darkness. The Whitechapel Paranormal Society was a flaming sword of light and hope, the final line of defense for Queen, country, and humankind.

Did you enjoy Craven Street?

If you enjoyed this book and would like to read more from the Whitechapel Paranormal Society series, please write a review.

Want to read more about the demon Forneus?

Begin the Ivy Granger Psychic Detective series now.

Learn more at IvyGranger.com.

Keep reading the Whitechapel Paranormal Society series.

Order Eeper Weeper now and continue reading the Whitechapel Paranormal Society series. Want a sneak peek? Keep reading for a sneak peek of the first chapter of Eeper Weeper and One for Sorrow.

Learn more at WhitechapelParanormal.com.

Sneak Peek: Eeper Weeper

"I didn't hear you come in, my dear," Doctor Hadley said, looking up from his paperwork.

"You were quite engrossed in your work, father," I said.

It was true. Doctor Jameson Foster Hadley was always obsessed with documenting the progress, or failures, of his latest experiments. He was driven by what he claimed was his duty to God and crown and all humankind. He would solve the mysteries of the human brain and fix all that he saw as evil and flawed in the many patients who filled the asylum outside these office walls.

"Are you wearing the shoes that I bought you?" he asked, eyes narrowing as he scrutinized the lower portion of my dress, as if he could force the fibers to part with his will and show him whether or not I had indeed offended him.

I went rigid, every muscle tensing as I prepared myself for what might follow. I was wearing the shoes in question, but I'd forgotten to screw the metal plates back onto the bottom of each shoe, a mistake that could be seen as dangerous rebellion, or worse. I forced breath into my lungs and bowed my head dutifully to the man I now called father, the man who was my salvation and my greatest enemy.

I chose my words carefully all too aware of what this monster was capable of.

"I am sorry, father," I said, casting my eyes to the floor. "I reached for my old shoes out of habit. It won't happen again."

"No, I dare say it won't," he said, piercing me with his gaze.

I held my breath, waiting for him to call for the orderlies to take me to the basement where I'd be subjected to endless questions. There would be no comfort, no food, no sleep within the stone walls of my father's laboratory. But fatigue and hunger were not the worst of my fears. I'd faced that much on the streets after my parents died.

It was what came after, when I was weak and tired and restrained, that was what turned my blood to ice in my veins.

I focused on the mundane sensation of pain where my corset dug into my ribs on one side. The bruise that blossomed there was just one more black mark upon my character. Doctor Jameson Foster Hadley had quite particular views on proper womanly behavior, and deep inhalations were not to be tolerated by the fairer, weaker sex. Indeed, as with the metal plates on my shoes to warn of my presence, the poor fit of my corset was calculated with the utmost scientific precision.

I knew all of this to be true. For although I'd often questioned what was real and what was delusion since entering the asylum's unscalable walls, the proof of my treatment plan was all around me. My father had dedicated fifty-one percent of his office—such a large amount of space when one considers the number of unfortunate souls under his care—to the charts, diagrams, and sketches of the devices and techniques currently in use upon my person.

But even more terrible were the detailed sketches for the procedures and gadgets that loomed in my future like a scalpel held aloft in the operating theater. Before my parents' deaths, I'd believed that knowledge held the power to dispel fear and worry. The good doctor's diagrams, always in full view, were evidence of my childish innocence. Knowing and anticipating the horrors to come was much worse than any level ignorance, no matter how low.

So I focused on the pain below my breast and tried to empty my mind. Whatever was to come would come. It was best not to think on it.

"My dear, I am disappointed, but you say that you put on the incorrect shoes out of habit," he said, tapping his desk with the tip of an ink stained finger. "I would not wish to alter this behavior too greatly, not when habit and routine are the greatest methods by which we can restore the damaged mind."

I risked a quick glance from his hands to his face, tears rising unbidden to join the hope that swelled inside my bruised chest. Had I truly escaped from this encounter unscathed? I measured my breathing by the ticking of the brass clock atop the mantelpiece before responding. A misstep now would destroy the limited goodwill my earlier comment had earned.

“I am sorry, father,” I said. “I will build a new habit with the shoes you’ve bought me.”

“And these new shoes, are they quite comfortable?” he asked.

My hand tightened into a fist at my side, but I kept my tone even as I replied, “The shoes only pinch if I walk quickly…which I know only from when I hastened to put out my light at the scheduled hour.”

He nodded, a satisfied smile on his lips as he made a notation in his ledger. I fixed the docile gaze of a dutiful daughter onto my face and waited for him to blot the page. Finally, he looked up from his desk and gestured for me to take the tray of discarded tea things, which had been the reason for this visit inside his domain.

But as I moved forward, he caught my wrist.

“If you promise to be good, I’ll let you join the patients in the garden,” he said, eyes alight. “You will be good, won’t you, Josephine?”

“Yes, father,” I said.

I would behave, but I daren’t hope that I would ever be good again. All that was right and true and innocent had died in the fire that killed my family. But I’d learned how to survive, first on the streets and now under the care and tutelage of my benefactor. I was his ward and I’d learned to do his bidding. I created a façade of grace, calm, and benevolence, but Doctor Hadley was a perceptive man. He’d made studying anomalous behavior his life’s work, which made him a difficult man to fool.

But I would pretend to be good, and hope that news of my “episodes” did not reach him. So far, I’d managed to bribe the staff with cakes and other sweets that I’d saved from my supper. I was too thin already, so I could scarcely afford to give them up, but without a means of bribery, I was as good as ruined.

I was the doctor’s success story. He’d taken me in and made a proper woman out of me, driving out ill habits and unsuitable behavior with various experimental therapies.

My tongue stuck to the roof of my mouth as I cleared away the morning’s dishes from his desk. He turned back to his work, dismissing me from his presence. I was once again unremarkable, a fixture in the room. If I were lucky, oh so lucky, I would remain that way. To be in that man's notice was a position so dire, I'd not wish it on the lowliest sinner, no not even the Devil himself.

I moved steadily to the door, practice and determination the only thing keeping the tea things from shaking noisily on the tray. I bit my lip and slid the door open wider, careful not to open it past the point at which it creaked.

I knew all the sounds of this room, all the whispers, moans, and cries of this entire rambling monstrosity of an estate. From the kitchens to the basement laboratories to the endless, winding halls of cell doors, this place was my home and my prison.

It didn't matter that I was the doctor's adopted daughter and not an inmate. My actions were just as scrutinized, my freedom just as limited. I was an ongoing experiment in a fancy hat and pretty dress.

If I was to survive, then I had to keep the doctor from learning the truth. I had to keep secret the thing the staff had already begun whispering about in the shadows. The great and prestigious man of science, Doctor Jameson Foster Hadley had somehow made a mistake. I wasn't good and I wasn't normal.

His experiment had failed.

Sneak Peek: One for Sorrow

The slogoth demon scuttled down the alley with inhuman speed. Its skittering claws echoed off the damp stone and brick storage buildings. There wasn't much wood this close to the water. The Thames ate everything over time, but it could soften wooden timbers to porridge in less than three London winters, rotting a building's body and stripping the flesh from its bones.

Much like the demon was doing as it emerged from its human host, the slap-slap of the putrefied remnants of the human girl hitting the cobbles punctuating its rapid retreat.

"I forgot how rudding fast these buggers can move," Flan said, flashing her teeth in what counted for a grin.

Edith managed a prissy grunt of disapproval, and I shook my head. So much had changed, but some things would always remain the same. Flan still swore enough to make the dock laborers who worked this district blush scarlet. Good thing those scarred and calloused men were asleep in their beds. There wouldn't be much honest activity down this part of Whitechapel until dawn, making this a prime location for demonic activity.

Demonic activity.

I shook my head again, this time a smile tugging at my lips. I'd left this life behind. We all had.

But for the first time in three years, I allowed myself to admit that I missed my old job of protecting the realm from paranormal threats. I loved the thrill of the hunt, and the sense of purpose, even if tracking down monsters meant having to put up with Edith St. Germaine.

"Angels save us, you are both enjoying this," Edith said, biting off the words. "Don't try to tell me otherwise. I always could tell when you girls were lying."

She could too. That was the rub. We all had minor psychic talents, skills that made us a formidable team, when we weren't fighting like rabid badgers dressed in crinoline.

When our unit was still together, we managed to work past our personal differences most of the time. Our task was vital to the survival of the realm, and we each took our orders, at least indirectly, from the Queen. But three years ago, Queen Victoria and her advisors had deemed our task complete.

The Special Paranormal Research Branch, a secret group of talented men and women working within the British police force, was created to monitor and gauge paranormal threats. I was part of an all-female unit with a success rate so high that we'd had more than one letter of gratitude from the queen.

The S.P.R.B. was headquartered in Whitehall, strategically located near Scotland Yard and the Cabinet Office, but our unit's high success rate was due in part to our willingness to chase down the leads that so often led to the unsavory streets of Whitechapel.

It seemed only right, our worlds coming full circle, that we now stood facing a demon in a putrid Whitechapel alley that stank of rotting fish and urine. Not that I'd had any hint that the paranormal would rear its ugly head into my life again.

I let out a heavy sigh. It had taken over two years to believe the reports, but I'd finally cast aside the unhealthy, obsessive level of vigilance that had become the all-consuming part of my life. I'd stopped listening for omens and portents, given up on the daily search through the newspapers, and no longer eyed every man on the street with suspicion. Cold drafts and strange odors had become benign details, no longer worthy of note.

There had been no more strange encounters with the paranormal. Ghosts, vampires, shapeshifters, and demons had gone quiet. Whether they were truly gone from this world or their hunger for power, mischief, and human blood lay dormant was a mystery—until today.

It was only an awkward attempt by Edith to save the darkest souls from our old team, those of me and Flan, over tea that had led us on this merry chase. I suppose when this was all over, I'd have to thank the lickspittle twit for that. Wouldn't that put Flan's bloomers in a bunch.

We'd come along for the free food and to get a rise out of Edith "I know you are lying" St. Germaine. Instead of tea and a tongue lashing, our afternoon consisted of trailing a shop girl who was demonstrating the telltale signs of demonic possession. We tracked her hoping that the demon riding the girl would lead us to a demon nest, or give us some hint of what Hell was planning.

Because if there was a slogoth demon prowling the streets of London, you could bet your ascot that there were more monsters lurking in the dark. Slogoth demons are nasty creatures, but they're not the brightest. No, someone or something else was controlling the demon.

But so far all we managed to deduce was that the demon had a sweet tooth for sugared biscuits, and sewer rats, and anything else she could get her hands on. It was Edith's indignant gagging during the demon's last snack, a seagull rotting in the gutter amidst a swarm of flies, that alerted the slogoth to our presence. Then the human body began to bubble and blister, and the demon ran.

Afternoon tea had served us up a demon. My heart raced and Flan let out an unfeminine snarl. It looked like our unit of the Special Paranormal Research Branch had one last job to do.

Order now to keep reading One for Sorrow.

Whitechapel Paranormal Society Series

Eeper Weeper

The great and prestigious man of science, Doctor Jameson Foster Hadley had somehow made a mistake. I wasn't good and I wasn't normal. His experiment had failed.

The tedium and terrors of Josephine "Jo" Hadley's existence within the stone walls of London's Bethnal Asylum are interrupted by a strange visitor, Cora Drummond, a woman who demands to interview one of the asylum's most insane residents. The patient's rantings include tales of ghosts and demons, but it is the bizarre, near-riotous muttering of prophetic nursery rhymes that follow Jo throughout the asylum wards that is most illuminating to Miss Drummond.

Eeeper Weeper, chimney sweeper. Had a wife, but couldn't keep her...

Days later, Jo and her adoptive father receive an invitation to attend an exclusive tea at the prestigious Whitehall Club. But the request for Jo's attendance is more than it might seem. She has caught the attention of a secret branch of government working directly for the queen.

Will Jo Hadley's unusual talent for inciting prophetic nursery rhymes prove useful to the crown? She is given one chance to demonstrate her worth to the Special Paranormal Research Branch, but this is one mission that even the most highly trained operatives might not survive.

One for Sorrow

Afternoon tea had served us up a demon.

It is six years since Josephine "Jo" Hadley joined the ranks of the Special Paranormal Research Branch and three years since the S.P.R.B.'s mission was terminated. After their superiors declare that the supernatural threat is quelled, Jo and her colleagues returned to civilian life with varying degrees of success. But when Jo, Edith, and Flan cross paths with a slogoth demon there is no escaping the terrible truth. The supernatural threat was never defeated.

One for sorrow. Two for mirth. Three for a funeral. Four for a birth. Five for Heaven. Six for Hell. Seven for the Devil, his own self.

Demons and necromancers went into hiding within the labyrinthine warrens of Whitechapel, but after three years of secretly feasting on the souls of London's East End they are back stronger than ever before. Will the Whitechapel Paranormal Society rise up from the ashes of the S.P.R.B., or will all of London become the Devil's playground?

Learn more at WhitechapelParanormal.com.

About the Author

E.J. Stevens is the bestselling, award-winning author of the IVY GRANGER, PSYCHIC DETECTIVE urban fantasy series, the SPIRIT GUIDE young adult series, the HUNTERS' GUILD urban fantasy series, and the WHITECHAPEL PARANORMAL SOCIETY supernatural mystery series. She is known for filling pages with quirky characters, bloodsucking vampires, psychotic faeries, and snarky, kick-butt heroines. Her novels are available worldwide in multiple languages.

BTS Red Carpet Award winner for Best Novel, Raven Award winner for Best Urban Fantasy, Imadjinn Award winner for Best Short Story, Independent Audiobook Award winner for Best Short Story, SYAE finalist for Best Paranormal Series, Best Novella, and Best Horror, winner of the PRG Reviewer's Choice Award for Best Paranormal Fantasy Novel, Best Young Adult Paranormal Series, Best Urban Fantasy Novel, and finalist for Best Young Adult Paranormal Novel and Best Urban Fantasy Series.

When E.J. isn't at her writing desk, she enjoys dancing along seaside cliffs, singing in graveyards, and sleeping in faerie circles. E.J. currently resides in a magical forest on the coast of Maine where she finds daily inspiration for her writing.

Connect with E.J. on Twitter @EJStevensAuthor.

Get fabulous freebies and stay connected at www.EJStevensAuthor.com.

Never miss a book release, giveaway, or a chance to hang out with E.J. Stevens at a live event.

Want a free book? Sign up for **E.J. Stevens' Newsletter** for exciting news, giveaways, free reads, and reader exclusives! http://www.subscribepage.com/n6k1a5

www.ingramcontent.com/pod-product-compliance
Lightning Source LLC
LaVergne TN
LVHW010105110826
845155LV00028B/493

* 9 7 8 1 9 4 6 0 4 6 3 6 9 *